CALLING THE DEVIL PARTNER

The Redemption of Howard Marsh 6

Bob McGough

Bearded Bard Inkworks

www.beardedbardinkworks.com

This arc of the Jubal County Saga could be called
Found Hope.
So each part is dedicated to a different group who helped
me find my Hope as an author.

To the folks who published me,
back when I used a different name.
You gave me my first break,
and were the first to take a gamble on me.
The first outsiders to tell me I had written something
worth selling, even if not for very much at all
Remind me not to take you to the casino.

Contents

An Introduction to Howard Marsh

Howard Marsh is a lot of things: a liar, a thief, a poor man's wizard. He's a shoddily tattooed skin stretched over a too skinny body that's barely held together by the same drugs that are tearing his life apart. A cynic, his words are often as poison as the substances he takes to pass his days, a suicide attempt years in the making.

He's the scion of a family with a history as rich as it is materially poor. He's the product of a miserable county with more dirt roads than paved, where poverty and loss is the order of the day. He's a man haunted by his past, and has yet to find any reason to try and piece himself back together.

You would be well advised to take what he says with a large grain of salt. He will cover the worst parts, glossing over the bits that show his darkest sides. The bits where the drugs that ravage him are in control. Where we find him is at the bottom, eking out a living as a water witch, a copper thief, a finder of lost things. Living in a storage shed and trying to maintain what's left of his frayed relationships with the few family members who will still talk to him.

But dear readers, he's a better man than he thinks. He doesn't see it; he's long forgotten the possibility even, and no one left in his life sees it either. But, if you can endure the miserable existence of watching someone make nothing but bad choices for a time, then you will perhaps be rewarded. Maybe you will see him slowly scrabble out of the muddy, trash filled ditch that is his life.

It won't be quick, and it won't be painless. The stories to come are often filled with sadness. The fairytale ending is not for stories such as these. There is a chance at happiness, but it is a long way away, and there are many obstacles both in him, and in his path.

This is not a plea for understanding, or forgiveness, or any sort of justification. It is just the way of things.

He is Howard Marsh, the Methgician.

And he doesn't give a damn what you think.

Mississippi Mayhem

*Being the Eleventh Tale in the Redemption of
Howard Marsh*

For Evan's Sake

The metal of the old Ford was warm under my arms. Leaning there against Evan's beat-up truck felt pretty pleasant, if I was being honest with myself. I mean, I was ready for the man to hit the road and quit bothering me, but it was a rare summer day in Alabama that wasn't just absolutely brutal with heat. A little breeze was blowing through my hair, and the sky was about as blue and perfect as a body could ever ask for.

The other man was tall—a lot taller than me, in fact—with the sort of wiry muscles farm boys tend to have. A worn Alabama shirt over some ragged stained jeans, a size or two too large, hung on his frame, and even though we were about the same age, he had a face about as lined and rough as mine. We'd both done more than our fair share of hard living.

Evan was drumming his hands lightly against the metal, his eyes kindly drifting over the assorted detritus that covered the bed. He was the sort who could never sit still, it seemed like, always tapping or making some kinda noise. Mostly I could just see half-crushed beer cans and sun-rotted plastic lures, but there were a trio of mighty fine fishing rods there as well, which were the center of attention at the moment.

"You sure I can't get you to come on, go fishin' with me? Day like today, we'll have a mess of bream in a half hour, tops."

Now, I'm not morally opposed to fishing or the like. In fact, I sorta like it, and I certainly am a fan of eating the proceeds. But sometimes I got in the mood where I could only take Evan in small doses. And even though I was feeling mighty sorry for the boy, I really just wanted to enjoy the day by myself. Well, and with a few drugs.

I scratched my chin. "No, not today. Iff'n it rains tomorrow like they say it's gonna, I might go with you then."

Evan nodded, straightening up and pushing away from the truck. "May just take you up on that. Gotta get while the gettin' is good."

He wasn't referring to the weather. The whole point of his visit was to come pick my brain about time in prison, seeing as he was looking down the barrel of a damn long stint in a couple of weeks. Luckily for me, I'd never done time as hard as what he was looking at, having spent all my behind-bars excursions in the Jubal County Jail. Prison was as foreign a beast to me as it was to him.

The sound of a large engine slowing to turn into the yard of storage sheds caught our attention just then. Heads turning, we watched as a Frito-Lay chip truck rocked and wobbled its way off the road and onto the gravel. Seeing as there were no snack machines in the U-Store-It, this was the kind of sight to properly catch my attention. Then I saw who was driving it, and my stomach sank.

"Is that Black . . . is that your daddy?" Evan asked, his voice more than a little incredulous.

"Fuck me if it isn't," I swore. Thomas Marsh—or Black Tom, as everyone tended to call him behind his back—was perhaps the biggest bastard in the whole county. And of course, just my luck, he had to be my dad. I hadn't even known he was out of jail and now here he was, sure as shit ramping up to ruin my day.

"Well, I think I'm gonna be getting on, then," Evan said abruptly, opening the door to his truck. "Thank ya for your time, Marsh, and lemme know 'bout tomorrow."

Before I could respond, the tall man was already inside the cab and cranking the truck. I stepped back from the tailgate and moved into the doorway of my shed, giving Evan plenty of room to get out of the line of fire, as it were. That chip truck could only move so fast, and by the time it pulled up into the spot where Evan's truck had been moments before, my friend had already turned onto the paved road, headed for safety.

There was no denying that we were related. The man who got out of that chip van was maybe an inch taller, but his hair was just as black, his eyes just as blue. I would say his eyes were kinda dead looking, but then I am biased by a whole lot of hate. Plus, he had a prominent beard, full and thick, as opposed to my three-day-old stubble. The prison tattoos, though, they looked about as quality as my own jailhouse ink, only a bit more splotchy with age and wear. The Frito-Lay uniform, however . . . that was new. And wildly out of sync.

"Was that Evan Brolin I saw go peelin' outta here?" my dad spat.

"Yeah," I offered, making no move to welcome the man.

"He owes me some money."

I didn't bother asking for what. If you owed my daddy money, it was almost certainly for something illegal. He wasn't anything resembling an honest businessman. "Well, you better go after him. Another week or so he'll be in Easterling, I reckon."

That brought a smile out of the ol' man, and it wasn't something pleasant. "I got buddies there. I'll get it out of him one way or the other. What he want with you?"

"Asked me about life inside. Wanting to be ready, I suppose." I wanted to ask why he was even here, but I was also hoping that if I never asked, maybe, just maybe, he'd ride on and leave me alone.

"Boy's soft. He ain't gonna do well." He looked back from the road and locked eyes on me. "Now, get your stuff together. We're taking a trip, me and you."

"Excuse me?" I surely was not expecting that. To be hit up for money? Sure. To have some of my drugs stolen? Probably. But a road trip with a man who'd be flabbergasted if he'd ever heard of the concept of a family vacation? Not on my radar, that's for sure.

His face quickly turned into a snarl. "Get your shit, and let's get on the road. We need to be in Mississippi tonight, and we gotta get this truck loaded first."

I stood there a second, then turned and stepped into my shed. I will argue with cops, judges, and Rutherford till the cows come home, but you did *not* argue with Black Tom, not unless you wanted to feel his boots connecting with your face. Over. And over. And over. And as I did not want to once again go through a Tom-issued ass-whoopin', I scooped up a backpack.

"How long am I packing for?" I asked, putting my box of oblivion down at the very bottom of the bag and throwing a couple shirts on top. I poured out some cat food out for Horace, my possum familiar, who was like as not digging through the Dairy Queen dumpster for snacks at this very moment. It would be enough to last him till Sunday, I hoped.

"One day down, one day for you to do what you do, then one day back. That's the plan, at least."

So, back on Saturday. I straightened. "'What I do'? You mean you ain't just bringing me along to move heavy shit?"

My daddy frowned, then spat. "More like *remove* some heavy shit this time. Like Mama does."

Shit.

Blues for 'Bama

"What's with the truck?" I asked as we rolled down 87.

Tom got a sly grin on his face, one that showed off just how rotted his teeth were getting. "You ever in your life see a chip truck pulled over by the cops?"

I thought for a second. "No, I reckon not."

"Exactly," he laughed. "Ol' boy who works at the shop where they fix these things, he owed me a favor. So, I got this till Monday. He even scored me one of the uniforms."

"I take it I'm not the only cargo we're looking to haul, then."

"You are not," he said, slowing to turn down Dannon Stand Road.

Silence took over then as we bounced and jostled down the dirt road toward Daddy's place. This wasn't where I'd grown up—that home was a burned-out shell over near my Granny's. This was where he'd moved to about ten years ago, right when he first got out of his first little stint in prison. I'd only been here rarely, and never of my own volition. It just didn't do to spend much time around the man.

The road was short, only a couple of miles, and really it was more of a driveway than anything. There was only one other home besides his, a tiny little farmhouse we passed by about halfway. An old man was sitting on the porch overlooking an overgrown yard, leaning against the oxygen tank he'd affixed to his walker. He gave a little wave and I nodded back, but I doubted those rheumy eyes saw it.

A half dozen dogs came running up as we pulled into the drive, barking up a storm. They were a rangy-looking mob of mutts, a little too thin, their eyes a little too hungry. But they shut right up when Daddy stepped out of the chip truck, running up to encircle him with their tails just a-wagging. They mostly ignored me except for one, who ran up with her tail tucked a bit to try and lick my hand.

"Out in the shed there's a half dozen cocks in boxes. Bring them on and set them by the back. I'll be getting the 'shine."

I sighed. That was how Daddy made most of his money. He bred fighting roosters, sometimes even the odd fighting dog or two, and made some damn good bootleg moonshine. I was fine with the liquor, but the rest of it turned my stomach. I loved animals mostly, and fighting them was real fucking wrong, I thought.

Walking across a yard more red clay than grass, I made it to the little tin shed and scooped up a pair of boxes. I could hear the roosters inside clucking away and felt the weight shift in the boxes as they moved around. I talked softly to them, trying to let them know it was gonna be ok, but if it had any effect at all, I sure couldn't tell.

I reached the back of the truck about the same time as Daddy. He had a milk crate in each hand, each filled with four gallon jugs of clear liquid. Opening the back doors of the truck, he placed them inside and reached out for my load, talking all the while.

"I was gonna take this load-a 'shine down to Troy first. Those frat houses, they'll buy up a good dozen cases between 'em, sometimes more. But last time I was there, some nancy boy asked if I could bring 'em fuckin' apple pie 'shine. Who the fuck ever heard-a such stupid shit? I'll be damned if I'mma sell them my good shit anymore. I'll take them a truckload of shit I get from the blacks—they can have that. Buncha damn pussies."

He glanced over at me. "Best thing I ever did, lettin' you drop outta school. Woulda plum ruint you."

I rolled my eyes. "Oh, yeah, done wonders for my career prospects."

Daddy set the rooster box down and casually backhanded me. I spun, my vision going white as the back of his hand struck my jaw. Pain flashed through my head, and I felt my lips split as I crashed to the ground.

I lay there for a second, stunned, but the man was already back to loading the van as though nothing had happened. The casual dismissal hurt my pride more than his hand had hurt my jaw, the fact that he knew he had to make no move to defend himself from reprisal. He'd beaten retaliation out of me decades ago.

Sitting up, I wiped my hand across my mouth and it came away with a bit of blood. Working my jaw a little, it popped, but nothing was broken at least. There would be a headache soon, I had no doubt, but I had stuff that would handle that well enough in my bag.

Without another word, I stood and went back to get another armload of roosters. *Nothing like a little casual violence to motivate the workforce.*

The Still, Silent Moments

My father is the scariest man I have ever met. He's supremely unsettling to be around, even if you don't know about his ever-present, barely suppressed violence. And it's mostly because of how fucking *still* he is.

If you ever run into the man, watch him. There's not one wasted movement. When he stands, he stands perfectly still. You have to watch close to even see him breathe. It gives you the feeling of some sort of wildcat getting ready to pounce. Even though he's still, oh so fucking still, there is always a feeling of energy waiting to spring loose. Like at any moment he could pull his pistol, or knife, and get to making mayhem.

Which he could. And historically has, more often than not.

This was the first time in years I'dseen him not wearing his pistol—I supposed because it wouldn't fit in with his disguise. Jubal County was one of those places where the sheriff had the discretion to not issue a pistol permit if he thought the person might be a danger to themselves or others. No sheriff in their right mind would ever have given my daddy a pistol permit, but he had not a care in the world. Even though he was a frequent flier felon and thus not allowed to have a gun, no law enforcement in the county was itching to have that fight. Some things were best left alone, I reckoned.

So, his revolver sat between us, resting on top of his overnight bag. You ever hear someone say "Oh, I keep a revolver 'cause I don't want it to jam when I need it," but you know deep down that's just them talking hard, trying to sound like a badass? You know good and well that when the rubber hits the road they're the type, like as not, to wet themselves. Well, with Black Tom, that was not the case. He also liked them big, heavy, and Western looking. Partly because deep down inside, I think he thought of himself as some sort of cowboy, but mostly because when he pistol-whipped someone with it, they tended to stay down after.

We rode north toward Montgomery at first, but pretty quick-like turned left and started making our way through Selma, then Demopolis, then through real West Alabama. If you ain't ever been out that way, let my save you the trouble: there ain't much there. Just spend your time going elsewhere unless you have a thing for history.

There were some real old houses out that way and some battlefields and the like, not that we were stopping.

Black Tom was not exactly a history buff. Even if he did have what was perhaps the most vulgar rebel flag tattoo you could imagine inked over his heart. Most flags I'd seen didn't have anatomy, much less genitals, but my father did have the occasional creative streak . . . even if it was horribly misplaced.

There are a lot of fields, cotton and peanuts mostly. Some catfish farms, too, which . . . well, I'd be lying if I said they didn't make me a little nervous. I half expected to see a giant catfish head broach up out the water and come calling, but luckily that wasn't the case. In fact, the most interesting sight I think I saw till we reached the state line was an old Ford truck with a truly astronomical number of wooden pallets stacked in the bed.

Tom, as you might imagine, was not much of a conversationalist, and there was no CD player in the chip truck—not even a radio, which I don't think should be legal. All we had to listen to was the engine and the wind, and while they can build up a certain cadence that could be relaxing, it's hard to relax with that big pistol just a-lyin' there beside you. There was also the occasional squawk from our feathered friends in the back, but they were surprisingly sedate, to the point that I wondered if Dad had drugged them in some way.

We did share a fat joint—out of my stash, mind you, even though I know good and well he had more *and* better weed than I did. But that was about as "father and son" as we got, which, if you think about it, is exceptionally tragic, so I did my very best to not think about it. I had other things on my mind.

Mostly it was hunger. Fuck me, but I was hungry, and damned if that truck didn't just reek of chips. I'd not so much skipped breakfast as forgotten to eat it, and now with it rocking on well into the afternoon, I was feelin' it. We passed by a couple dozen fast food joints, all told, but did we stop? Fuck no. Daddy had a weird thing against fast food, so I knew better than to even try and ask. I just had to hope he'd notice me withering away into noth-ingness, or that the steady rumble of my stomach would finally drown out the engine noise.

You would think that a chip truck might have some snacks lying around, but that was not the case unless I wanted to eat some very, very raw chicken. And of course, smoking that weed helped not one iota and, in fact, just tacked some munchies onto my starvation. I was dream-ing of mutiny, even if I knew I wouldn't ever make that move.

So, I spent some of my time texting Anna. The girlfriend was none too pleased that it was looking like I would be gone most of the weekend, as that was the only time we ever saw each other. In truth, that had me rightly bummed out as well. I was mighty attached to that tall drink of water, more than I had been with any woman in years. Maybe ever, if I were being honest.

We didn't get to talk too much, though, as she was at school and mostly caught up in her classes. Neither one of us were big on talking on the phone, but I told her I'd try and give her a call sometime tomorrow, whenever she was done with her schoolin' for the week. I didn't make no promises, though, and when I told her why Daddy had picked me up, she understood. She hadn't met my dad before, but she'd heard enough stories.

Eventually we crossed into Mississippi, my first time in the state. It was only the third state I had ever visited, besides a couple spring break-style trips down to the panhandle of Florida. I liked to travel, but travel costs money, and money was usually best spent on other more local diversions. Right there I decided that if I survived my bout with starvation, I was going to make the most of this trip.

East Mississippi was visually no different from West Alabama, which was both disappointing and reassuring. Lots of bullshit pine trees, lots of fields, more than a few cows, some catfish ponds. The houses were just as poor, for the most part, and if it wasn't for there being a few more cedar trees than I was used to seeing, it could've been just another part of Jubal County.

"Hungry, boy?" Tom asked, glancing my way. Before I could really answer, my desiccated tongue being hardly up to the task of talking just then, he was already turning into the yard of a little BBQ joint.

Earl's Real Pit BBQ wasn't real big, and it was clearly pretty old, but in that moment it was the most beautiful place on earth. I could've kissed its weathered clapboard siding, and each breath I took in was filled with the smell of woodsmoke coming up from the pit around back. Judging from the number of cars and trucks in the fairly small parking lot, the place was popular.

"I could eat," I managed to squeak out from a mouth that I wasn't totally sure didn't have drool leaking out of it. "But I ain't got no money on me, so you payin'?" In truth, I did—a little—but I was aiming to milk the man as much as possible for my trouble.

Dad grunted, an angry sound, but after a moment he gave a little nod. "Literally eating into my profits this trip, boy."

I could have pointed out that he was the one who brought me along and had, in fact, opened my mouth to do just that when I remembered he'd just agreed to pay for my food. With a temper like his, it was best to jump on any glimmer of kindness whenever they appeared. It would be a few years, at best, before you got another.

He pulled the chip truck onto the grass on the edge of the parking lot, there not being a space big enough for him to squeeze into. With an almost pained expression he placed his pistol beneath his seat, then got out. I was right behind him, careful not to get too close. You know, just in case.

Compared to how bright it was outside, within Earl's it was pretty near cave dim. Damn near every table looked to be full, though, and a few older ladies were scampering to and fro refilling drinks and the like. A glance to my left showed me that I could see back into the kitchen area, where an enormous fat man with a thick beard was wiping a greasy hand across his brow before going back to chopping pork. This was my kind of place.

"Janice" read the nametag of the gray-haired woman who sat us. The table was covered with a checkered plastic tablecloth, and she quickly wiped what looked like corn-bread crumbs away. That's when I learned that Dad had clearly been here before, as he quickly ordered a pair of "Big Earl's," which I learned were massive chopped pork sandwiches with fries and a sweet tea.

She brought us our teas a minute later while I was making every effort to look anywhere but at Tom. He was studying something on his phone, but it was getting to a level of awkward silence that not even I could stomach.

"So, what's this all about? Why you taking me to . . . where are you taking me, by the way?"

Daddy looked up from his phone, his eyes still sorta squinted. He needed glasses but wouldn't ever own up to it. "Grinwood, Mississippi. That's where we're headed."

"Never heard of it," I said.

He nodded slowly. "Don't reckon you had any reason to. Small place, not even a stoplight. But it's sorta in the middle of a lot of larger places, and a couple of decent roads blow through it. Gets more traffic than it should, for a place its size."

It was my turn to nod. Small places were exactly the sorts of locations he tended to operate in. The sort of place that had no local cops, just maybe the odd sheriff deputy. "So why we headed there?"

Tom breathed out heavily, a fairly angry sound. "I ain't looking to play twenty fucking questions all during dinner. My boss, I heard him talking about some fuckery, and I said I knew someone like as not could handle it—that's you. So, we're going to make my boss happy. He'll tell you all the details. Now shut up and leave me in peace."

Daddy was in the Dixie Mafia, so whoever his boss was would be someone higher up in that group. I'd managed to steer well clear of them over the years, except for my unwanted run-ins with Tom, but then I had nothing they wanted. Far as I knew, though, they had nothing to do with anything involving the sort of spooky shit my family typically found itself caught up in. Probably why my dad had joined up, come to think of it.

See, Daddy had not only inherited absolutely none of his parents' power—which isn't all that uncommon, really—he was also sort of the anti-power. Folks like the rest of my aunts and uncles, they got little hints of the power, like how Uncle HD knew when he was gonna get company or when he was needed, or like Uncle Rooster and his singing.

But with Daddy, not only did he get nothing—not even the faintest hint—but power wouldn't work on him at all. He was a sort of . . . null zone or something. And because of that, he hated it. With a passion, as not a few of my scars can attest to. Compared to Daddy, I'm a scrawny little shit who uses magic to even the score. When I can't use magic . . . well, then that score never gets even close to even.

Then Janice sat down a couple of food-filled plates in front of us, and the only sound was us chewing.

CLASSY

Daddy hadn't been lying about Grinwood. It was a thin slice of nothing sitting in the middle of a swampy nowhere. Pretty enough, the way some small towns are, but not much to take in.

We stopped at a small gas station, the kind of mom-and-pop place that most towns had long done away with. While Daddy gassed up the van, I took the time to smoke a cigarette and stretch my legs. There was a lazy yellow dog lying in the shade on the edge of the asphalt that kept one eye on me, giving the occasional wag of its tail. It seemed like it wanted me to come pet it but couldn't muster the energy to come to me. I saw a lot of myself in that dog.

Little bits of trash flitted in the breeze. A Hardee's bag, no doubt tossed by someone gassing up, was doing an admirable impression of a tumbleweed across the asphalt.

Some sort of flyer, maybe a missing poster, was flapping against the station door, the bits of tape holding it in place struggling mighty hard. It would be joining the Hardee's bag soon enough, I reckoned.

My phone had pretty much no service, flirting with one bar of signal at most. I wished I had one of them smartphones like Anna had so I could look up anything about this place, see if there was any news of note, but instead I just had to wander around to find enough signal to text her so she would know where I was. If I turned up missing, I knew she would take the time to let the proper authorities know, and hell, she would probably even make an effort to find me. Her, HD, and Krista.

I knew Daddy sure as hell wouldn't. In fact, odds were he'd be involved in some way.

The gas station sat at a crossroads. Daddy had been right; there wasn't a stoplight, but there was a four-way stop that saw a surprising amount of traffic. In truth, it probably could have used a stoplight, as a steady stream of cars and trucks threaded their way past the station. I leaned against the back of the chip truck and watched them pass, taking in everything from a rebel flag-painted jacked-up truck to a Sunkist-painted Caprice sittin' on what a sticker in the window said were twenty-four-inch rims. I didn't know if they was a full twenty-four, but they were shiny as hell, and that car was pretty damn badass. Love a Sunkist.

Five miles from the gas station, we turned down an old paved road. It looked as though it hadn't been worked on since it had been first laid down, and it had more than its fair share of potholes. This may come as a surprise, but them chip trucks don't have world-class shocks, so we were in for a bumpy ride. Those roosters in the back took up to squawking something fierce, and I couldn't say as I blamed them. Thankfully, Tom scooped up the pistol before it could fall into the floor and laid it across his lap.

It was getting on into evening, that gray time of the day when you can tell night ain't too far off. It was light enough that we didn't need headlights on, but on a few of the nicer cars we met, the type with automatic lights, they were starting to click on. The day had gotten away from me, I realized.

All around us were woods. They lined either side of the road, and though they weren't full-blown swamps, they were certainly nudging up on that line. A good rain or two and I was sure they'd be more mud than grass. In that moment, though, they were pretty enough, and I even spotted the odd firefly or two.

Ten miles or so outside of Grinwood, Daddy began to slow the chip truck down. We turned on to a dirt drive, but I was surprised to find it was in better shape than the damn paved road. It had a nice layer of gravel on it and was smoother than what we'd been traveling on by a good bit.

Maybe twenty yards down this road was a wooden archway, like something you'd see in a Western. "Lagniappe" had been burned into the wooden sign that hung down from it, the letters maybe a foot tall. I had no idea what it meant, but it looked sorta French, I thought.

I saw lights on up the road a bit, shining through the trees. They had a festive look about them, and you could tell some had begun their life as Christmas lights. Most were yellow-white strings of tiny bulbs like what might be in a small lamp, and in the rapidly falling dusk, they made quite a sight.

The road led to a clearing, a pretty good-sized one, at that. Someone had put a good chunk of money into the place at some point, raising it up out of that half-assed swamp and making a good level surface. A long, low building took up most of the space, and whatever that didn't occupy was being used by cars in a rough parking lot.

The building was wood, and the few windows I could see were mostly filled with neon beer lights advertising the staples like Bud Light and Corona. A big porch took up the whole front of the place, and you could see a bunch of picnic tables filling the area. A few folks were standing around, bottles in hand as they took pulls from lit cigarettes. Typical country folk, by the looks of things.

Daddy drove carefully around the parked cars and guided the beast down a little bit of a rutted path. The building made a bit of an *L* shape and, somehow managing to not hit a tree or slip off into the wannabe swamp, he got the thing around the back to where there was a bit of a loading dock. A couple of other big trucks and vans, all delivery-type vehicles, were parked around as well.

The big roll-up door at the loading dock was open, and a shirtless man with an immense potbelly was leaned up to one side. An unlit cigar filled the side of his mouth, its end chewed wet and ragged. After a few moments of watching Daddy park, he began lumbering toward us.

"Hey theyah, Tom," Big Boy said as the engine shut off. "Di'n't speck you back soon a' this." It was hard to tell whether his thick accent or the moist cigar was more of a contributor to how difficult he was to understand.

Daddy nodded to the man. "Greg, get a couple boys to unload me. I got fightin' cocks and 'shine."

"Sho thing," Greg replied, walking back toward the roll-up doors and yelling unintelligibly around his cigar. He had to hitch his pants up every dozen steps or so, making for a disgusting, if comical, sight.

"Boss's cousin," Tom spat as he started changing out of his ill-gotten uniform. "Fuckin' idiot."

I just stood there waiting, thankful I wasn't the one having to unload the truck. A couple of young men—barely out of high school, if I had to bet money—came and started hauling the moonshine inside the building. They were damn near twins, both just a set of too-tight jeans over well-worn work boots with back pockets worn almost through from where their dip cans rode. The only difference I could see was the color of plaid in their shirts.

A minute later Dad had on his usual black jeans and wifebeater, his pistol strapped to his side. He dug out a well-worn Stetson from the back—his favorite, the one with the rattlesnake hatband. I'd been there when he killed the thing, and Momma getting it turned into hat band had been the last Christmas present the Marsh household ever experienced.

The boys were back and, grabbing boxes of roosters, began heading not toward the building but out past the truck. There was a well-worn trail heading out into the woods, and squinting hard, I was pretty sure I could see a bit of tin out that way. At a guess, I reckoned that was where they kept the critters. I made a note of it, filing that snippet away. With Daddy around, it paid to keep a list of potential hiding places on tap.

"Come on," Tom said, slipping one of his big knives into his boot top. He straightened and began walking toward the building.

I followed along a couple steps behind as he took us in through the roll-up door into a small warehouse-type space. There was a shit ton of beer and the like—kegs, bottles, and cans, all of the good cheap types. I didn't see the moonshine we'd just brought, but then I had to imagine they didn't keep illegal shit just lying around in the open. There were too many signs of money here, and "big money" and "stupid" don't usually go together.

It was clean and felt sorta new. Everything I'd seen since coming to Mississippi had been pretty much like 'Bama—in short, not a lot of new. A space like this with clean concrete and tidy stacks of booze definitely stood out. It was enough to set a grubby man like myself on edge.

Passing through a doorway, I began to feel more at home. I realized that the warehouse space here, that must have been a fairly new add-on to what was a much older building. The hallway I was in now was all creaky wood boards and old pictures in dusty frames. It felt very mom-and-pop, which was a bit more my speed.

Tom stalked up to the only sign of life here—a large man in a Harley-Davison shirt who had a good foot and a half on Daddy, and might have been twice as wide—but it wasn't Daddy who turned away first from the little staring/pissing match the two got into. "He in there?" Tom finally asked, gesturing to the door the giant was clearly guarding.

Big Boy looked at Tom's gun. You could see him thinking about saying something, but once again, some fights ain't worth it. "Go on in. He's been waiting on you."

Tom didn't respond; he just opened the door and stepped inside. I followed close behind, not wanting to be left alone with the guy who could smack me into a drug-addled paste without breaking a sweat.

Act Like You Know

The next room was an office. It was nice—far nicer than the rest of the building I had seen, in fact. A thick dark-green carpet covered the floor and the furniture was all wood, and all fancy. I suspected they were all some sort of antiques, but I was far from an expert. For me, "age" usually meant dust and decay, not polish and shine.

A big ol' desk dominated the room, big enough that you knew they had to either assemble it in the room or build the entire space around it. Weren't no way it had fit through that door. It certainly drew the eye, and then sort of filled it up, but I couldn't focus on that. More pressingly, there was a man behind the desk.

He was fairly old. Older than my daddy, from the looks of things—maybe early sixties, with short-cut gray hair and a trim beard to go along with it. He had that weathered look of someone who'd done a lot of work outside when they were younger, but I had a sneaking doubt this man had done much in the way of heavy work in some time.

"Big" was one word that came to mind—big enough that the desk he lorded from didn't seem outsized. He was face down in some paperwork that looked to be a stack of invoices, but he looked up as we came in, leaning back into his chair as he did so. It creaked smoothly, a sound hard to describe. In a poorer chair it would have been a whiny squeak, but in whatever fancy chair he was in, it came out more proper sounding.

"Tom, back again." The man said it with a tone neither warm nor hard. Just stating facts, as it were.

I noticed for the first time there were no chairs across from the desk. Any office I'd ever been in, there were chairs for visitors like me to cop a squat in. Though there was a small couch to one side of the room, there was no place that it seemed like was actually *meant* for me to sit. Which, it quickly dawned on me, was very likely intentional. This man was either real unfriendly, or he liked wrong-footing folks.

Tom nodded. "Brought half my usual load, seeing as I didn't have time enough between runs to get up the usual."

"Will that cover your expenses?" the big man asked.

My dad jerked a finger toward me. "Barely. But I thought bringing him along might help mitigate that fact."

The other man had clearly seen me, but now he took notice of me. His dirt-brown eyes looked me over, a quick appraising glance. "Is this the man you were telling me about?"

Tom nodded. He looked like he wanted to spit but had no place to do so. The fact that he didn't just up and spit on the floor told me everything I needed to know about the man behind the desk. "Frank, this is my boy, Marsh."

Even my own dad failed to call me by anything other than my last name. I might as well have gone and cut the first half of my damn birth certificate right off. I'd have been annoyed if I wasn't so used to it. However, it was still odd to hear him claim me as his spawn.

I took a step forward and extended my hand. "Howard Marsh," I muttered. I wasn't usually one for formalities, but I could tell this was a man to be respected, and most likely feared. With cops, you're supposed to respect them just because they have a badge. That ain't always earned—that's given, which is why I never gave them the time of day unless it would fuck them over somehow. With a man like Frank, though, you could tell whatever he had, he'd earned. It paid to be on the right level with him.

A meaty, calloused hand engulfed mine, giving me a firm shake. There was no power play here; he didn't try to crush it or anything, but it was as solid a grip as you could ask for. "Frank Osmond," the man said in return.

Turning his large head back to my father, he nodded toward the door. "Go see John. He'll get you paid out."

Tom turned and strode out of the room without another word. If I didn't know any better, I would've thought the man was unnerved by something. Though, if I was being brought in for magic reasons, that made sense, I guess. Daddy only had two reactions when it came to spooky shit: stay away, or kill it with fire.

As the door clicked shut, Mr. Osmond turned his focus on me. "Your father there tells me you have a knack for solving unusual problems. As I have one of those, I thought perhaps we could come to an arrangement."

"Well, that depends on the problem," I said truthfully. Not everything can be fixed by magic, especially when you're as untrained as I am. "I can do a few things, but I tend to be more of a hammer than a scalpel, if that makes sense."

Frank nodded. "It does. Similar to the work I have your father do from time to time—he's not a subtle man. So, how about I tell you my problem, and you tell me if we can make something happen?"

"Sounds fair to me."

Frank started pulling a pack of cigarettes from the desk and went about lighting one as he talked. "Three of my guys have died in the past month and a half, all from tragic accidents. Just pure bad luck in each case—at least that's what it looks like. I would say I am an overly suspicious man by nature, but I would like to think anyone would agree that if three of their employees died in such a short amount of time, something was amiss."

"I think you'd be fairly right in that assessment." I wanted to sit down, but I hadn't been asked and, again, the only option was that low couch a good ways away. I shifted uncomfortably from one foot to the other, sort of overdoing it a bit to try and finagle an invite.

"The first, Jerome, he fell off his bass boat, hit his head, and drowned. He was with his wife, and she had zero reason to kill him, before you ask. The second flipped a three-wheeler and snapped his neck. He was a distant cousin of mine, bit of an idiot named Kerrie. And the last, just a few days ago, was Willy June." Frank leaned back in his chair, causing it to creak richly at the strain. "He left out of here and drove himself straight into a tree going about ninety. Explosion woke folks up miles away."

I nodded. "You reckon maybe he killed himself?"

"Willy? Kill himself?" The big man shook his head. "No, Willy wasn't smart enough to kill himself. I got this theory that only smart folks kill themselves. Which, a lot of folks would say that killing yourself is mighty dumb, but the way I figure it, natural preservation is about as ingrained in us as anything. You got to be smart enough to out-reason your instinct to do something like that. Willy? He was loyal, and he was tough. But I wouldn't trust him with anything more complicated than 'lift that' or 'hit him.'

"Besides, he had no reason, at least not that anyone knows. The boy was an open book, really. Never graduated high school, got a job moving furniture and bouncing on occasion till I took him on. Still lived at home with his momma. Had a few girlfriends, but nothing serious. He'd risen about as far in life as he was gonna and lived pretty well. He had no reason to complain."

"Well . . ." I shrugged. "I mean, can you ever really know someone? For all you know, he was a kiddie diddler or something."

"Sure. And if I hadn't seen what I saw, I probably would just chalk it up to something like that."

My eye arched. "What did you see?"

Frank picked up a remote from atop the desk and pointed it at the bank of small screens set up in the corner. "Here is where we come to the meat of the matter. Willy, his gas pedal got stuck somehow, which is how he wrecked. And the other two died real natural, if way early in life. And yes, sometimes weird coincidences happen, but when he died, I took it upon myself to look into things a little bit."

"Because you're a suspicious type," I offered.

"Exactly," he said, pressing Power, then Play on the remote.

The screen showed a room that looked like a fairly typical bar. I assumed it was the front part of the building we were standing in. I could see a few folks milling around with beers in their hand. Everything was in shades of black and white, but the image was as clear as could be, showing tables, chairs, a long bar, a dozen people, and to one side, roughly a half dozen slot machines.

A tall, thick man came onto the screen. "That's Willy," Frank said, gesturing to the figure. He was slowly making his way through the crowd, stopping briefly to slap one man on the back and say a few words. Then he was through the little knots of people and over by the slot machines. Moving down the row, he paused in front of the one on the very end and, sitting on the stool, fished out a bill from his wallet and put in in.

"Mr. Marsh, how many slot machines do you count?"

I did the quick math. "Seven. Six empty, and one with your boy in front of it."

"Sharp eyes. The problem is, though—and you can walk into the room as soon as you leave this office to confirm this—is that we only have ever had six slot machines here."

Planets Collide

"**W**ell, that ain't good," I muttered, staring at the screen.

"Yes. Watch." Frank began fast-forwarding the tape. The men and women moved in triple time, coming and going quickly across the camera's line of sight. Willy just sat there—for five minutes, the timer said, then ten, then finally, at around the fifteen-minute mark, Frank pressed Play once more.

The time returned to normal speed. Willy slammed his fist against the side of the slot machine, his face fairly angry. He stood up quickly, knocking the stool over as he did. He spun and kicked the stool and stormed off, making for the door.

"Willy didn't gamble much. He had a temper, so I had to make some rules that limited his playing when customers were around. He'd actually kept to them, near as I could tell, up until this." Frank looked away from the screen, watching me instead. "Now, watch close."

A tall gaunt man in a black cowboy hat came from around from behind the bar, walked over, and stood the stool back up. The moment he turned back, the screen went fuzzy. You could still see the picture mostly, but everything was hazy for about two seconds. When it cleared up, the slot machine was gone.

I whistled, low and long. "Well, again, that ain't good . . . though I suspect you could probably make some money selling this tape to the tabloids. Some expert would come out saying it was fake in a day or two, but at least you'd have a couple extra grand in your pocket."

Frank frowned. "I don't think so." His tone made it clear exactly what he thought of that idea. He struck me as a fairly private person, so that made sense, I supposed. As for me, I would love a couple grand. *So many drugs . . .*

The big man cut off the TV then. He leaned back slightly in his chair once more, steepling his fingers in front of him, his elbows on his desk. "So, what are we dealing with here? And what can you do about it?"

I kept my mouth closed for a moment, chewing the thought over in my head. That hazy flickering, that was magic doing something to the technology. A lot of times, those two things didn't mesh too well. The issue was, was it active magic, like someone casting a spell? Or that sort of passive magic like what a magical creature possesses?

"Well, could be a couple things. Maybe something like a trickster spirit, or a fairy. Maybe a ghost of some sort. It's hard to say, really. I'm guessing you talked to your people—they ever seen this thing before? You got it on tape any other time?"

Frank shook his head. "We only keep tape about a week at a time, so if it's cropped up in the past, I wouldn't know. No one says they've noticed anything weird, however."

"Anything like beer going missing, or maybe stuff that might seem like normal pranks? Maybe liquor going bad?" I had it in mind that maybe they'd pissed off some sort of house fey when they had built the warehouse add-on. Some older houses and structures still had those lurking around, though no one paid them any homage normally. Those traditions were long dead.

"No. I don't allow shenanigans. My employees know better, and I pay them well enough that they actually obey."

Well, there goes that idea, probably. I was out of my home turf, and I had no idea what the local mystical layout was like. I really could've used some inside information, but if Frank had known anyone with power locally, I suspect there wouldn't have been a need to bring me in. I tried another angle.

"These three guys, anything connect them other than working for you? Or would getting at them be a way to get at you?"

The big man's frown deepened. "If someone wanted to hurt my operations, there would be far better folks to deal with. Willy, Jerome, and Kerrie were low men on the totem pole. They made deliveries, collected . . . things, that sort of stuff. I have a dozen other men just like them, and there's always plenty more where they came from. Steady jobs don't grow on trees in Grinwood."

"So that's the only connection? Them working for you?"

"Well, they were all fairly close. They'd drink together on occasion, that sort of stuff. Them, Halley Cross, and Far-rel Thomason, they all played softball together, I think. Sort of a clique, if that makes sense."

Well, at least that was something to go on. "I guess I'll go take a look at the slot machines. And if you could, maybe make me a map or something so I can go look at the spot where the wreck was."

Frank nodded. "Sure. Do what you need to do, and if anyone asks, tell them I said they are to leave you the hell alone or help you out—whatever you need."

"Fair enough." I thought about raising the idea of some sort of compensation, but I knew that anything he paid me, Daddy would just take off me before we got home. So what was the point here? Still, I had it in mind to milk this for what I could. "I'll be back in a bit."

Stepping back outside, I had to walk around the absolute mountain guarding the door. He barely glanced at me, instead using his eyes to follow a passing brunette woman in a short skirt. She looked like she might be a waitress, or maybe a bartender, as she was wearing a pale-blue shirt that read "Welcome to the Lagniappe Lounge!"

I followed along after her, assuming that she would be making her way toward the bar area. It gave me time to marvel at the odd art on the back of that shirt. I thought the lazy-eyed gator was a nice touch, and I wondered if the offset eye was intentional or if they'd just had a shitty graphic artist. The crawfish, though, was a bit much. Why would you put boobs on a mudbug? Come on now.

Sure enough, after passing through a swinging double door, I found myself in what I guessed was the lounge area. I half expected sawdust on the floor, what with the country-western playing, but it was just a typical hardwood with decades' worth of spilled beer as a stain. The chairs around the tables all matched, which was truly the greatest wonder of the place, more so than a vanishing slot machine.

There were maybe a dozen folks in the bar, about half looking to be employees. They were mostly behind the bar, unloading bottles of beer and liquor into various coolers and the like. Judging from the activity, they were gearing up for quite a night.

Short Skirt walked behind the bar and I caught her attention for the first time. She had a nice face, warm and friendly, but looked tired. The makeup she was wearing, it seemed less to pretty her up—no need for that, I thought—but more to hide the very faint outline of what had been a nasty bruise on her cheek. Most folks wouldn't have noticed, especially in bar light, but then a lot of folks didn't have a momma like mine who'd had a lot of practice in covering black eyes.

I pushed that thought away and tried to focus on the task at hand. "Excuse me, Mr. Osmond said y'all was supposed to help me as I needed."

She pursed her lips. "Alright. I'm Teresa."

"Simple request for you, then, Teresa. Can I have a beer?" I gave my most winning smile, which no doubt showed off just how many missing teeth I had. First impressions are important.

"That's easy enough. Am I starting you a tab, then?"

"Oh, no, Mr. Osmond is paying."

She snorted. "If you say so. I gotta warn you, though, if you ain't actually on his tab, then you're gonna regret the sheer hell out of this, so make it a good one."

I felt confident that "have the employees help you" definitely covered free beer. And if it didn't, well, we'd cross that burning bridge as we came to it. "I'm a simple man, so let's go with a High Life." I winked.

With practiced efficiency, she had an ice-cold open bottle in my hand just a few heartbeats later. Before I could even thank her, she was already on the move farther down the bar, doing whatever it was busy people did. I shrugged and, taking a sip, strode over toward the slot machines.

THE FALLING VEIL

The slot machines were the brightest spots of light in the whole place. A row of six, they were the type that had digital screens instead of those rolling wheel thingies inside. They still had handles that could be pulled, it looked like, but it seemed that most everything was handled by the touch screen.

They all had their own theme. One was Western, another had a sort of Greek mythology vibe, another was all about safaris. Didn't matter what color lipstick you put on a pig—end of the day, it was still a pig. I guessed folks just liked to have different sets of colored lights to stare at as they lost their money.

Only one was in use at the minute. An old man sat there steadily tapping away, resting a small bucket of change on his ponderous gut. One hand did the gambling while the other alternated between sips of some sort of liquor and long pulls on a cigarette. He wasn't on the very end, but one down, so I decided I would try my best not to disturb him as I took a closer look.

The spot where I'd seen the phantom slot machine was, unsurprisingly, empty. I didn't even see an outlet in the wall that someone could use to plug a machine in, unless it was hidden out of sight behind the others. Which wasn't unlikely, I guess, but I knew better. *You don't have to plug in a spirit for it to work.* I did sort of make like I was looking at the machine closest to me, as if I was pondering doing some gambling of my own, but really I was reaching out with my senses, trying to sniff out something wonky.

I muttered a few low words under my breath. It wasn't a spell, exactly, but I hoped it would help put my mind right, sorta open it up to the world beyond. I was getting a little snippet of a feeling when a voice intruded.

"What was that?" asked the gambler from a couple feet away. He didn't bother so much as glancing in my direction, his eyes fixed on the screen in front of me.

I fumbled. "I, uh . . . is this one lucky at all?" I asked, gesturing to the machine I was nominally looking at.

The man gave a snort. It was so derisive that it said all that needed to be said. It was a stupid question, I supposed. If it had been lucky, the old bastard would've been sitting there instead. I went back to focusing my senses.

There was a lingering scent there. It took me a moment, but as I narrowed my attention it came to me. There was a spectral sort of stench of swamp mud. It was earthy, but also sort of soured. As if something had gone bad.

For a split second, less than a quick heartbeat, my eyes caught a glimpse of something. There was the faintest hint of a slot machine, but also so much more—that spot was a swamp, deep dark mud pooled around the base of a thick tree. There was a sound of shovels and sucking mud pulling at something, dragging it down.

And then it was gone.

I knew the feel of a ghost. I'd had more than my fair share of encounters with them, especially the kind that could cause trouble. Not that I usually ended up handling them—that was more the domain of my buddy Jeff Earl—but this had that feel about it, and had it in spades. There was nothing more I could do in that moment, not without more information or more privacy, so I walked away, leaving the old man back by his lonesome.

I finished my beer as I walked back to the bar and, setting the empty on the counter, I raised a hand to catch the eye of the woman from earlier. She took my empty and asked if I wanted another. Since I wasn't paying—at least not yet—the answer was, of course, a firm yes.

"You know Willy June?" I asked as she placed the new beer in my hand. It was delightfully cold.

She gave a little shrug. "Well enough, I guess. Not that we were friends, but sorta more work acquaintances. He worked out the warehouse, though, so we didn't see each other all that often. Sad what happened, though."

"Yeah, it is, at that," I said, trying to muster up some feeling I didn't have. "You working the night he died?"

She shook her head. "No, sorry. My kid had some sort of stomach bug, and I couldn't find a sitter who wanted to take the risk."

I nodded, then decided to cut to the chase. "Anything weird been going on?"

She paused, giving me a look. It was hard to read, but I could tell she was working the issue of me over in her mind, trying to put two and two together. She seemed like a smart girl, but she didn't have enough pieces to put together a full picture, I reckoned. After a moment, she answered, "No, nothing like what I think you might be getting at. There's always something odd going on—that's bar life for you. But nothing . . . *weird*. 'Least not that I've heard."

"Alright, then," I said, taking a step away from the bar. I tipped the beer in her direction. "Thanks much."

She gave me a hard look—not mean, just the kind that said she wasn't done puzzling me out. "Anytime," she said. She had a question in her eyes—I could see it, but after a moment she went back to her work, so I decided to go talk to Frank.

Babysitter

I told Frank he was dealing with a ghost and that I would try and handle it. He had me a map ready as well as a list of a couple names and numbers I might try. It was a start. I wasn't sure what all I could do without my usual connections, but it's not like I had anything better going on.

All told, about a half hour had passed since I'd last seen Tom. I found him in the warehouse counting out a small stack of bills. The man who'd handed it to him stood there with his arms folded across his black Dickie's work shirt. A moment later, Dad gave a curt nod and folded the money into his thick billfold. Work Shirt extended a hand to Tom, but that asshole just turned and started walking away into the evening light. I feel like a better person would have given the stiffed man an apologetic glance or word, but then I am my father's son to a degree, so I just followed after.

"Frank gave me a place to go check out. Can you take me there?" I asked.

Tom frowned. "Fuck no, I got work to do. I ain't your fucking chauffeur, and I sure as hell ain't gonna be around when you pull some Momma shit."

I stopped walking. My voice might have gotten a little loud, but then this had caught me by surprise, even if it probably shouldn't have. "Then what you reckon I'm supposed to do? Fucking walk?"

He whirled, getting in my face. His voice was low enough that only I could hear it, and it was chock-full of menace. "Listen here, you little shit. If you think I won't beat your ass right here in front of God and everybody, you are sorely fucking mistaken. Now, I called your cousin—he's on his way to get you. You're his problem now, and if you aren't back here and in the van by noon Sunday, well, I guess you just live in Mississippi now. So you handle your shit, I'll handle mine, and keep the fuck away from me."

He was a dozen feet away before my butt unpuckered and I could think clearly again. "Cousin?" I asked, befuddled as hell. I don't know if I didn't say it loud enough or if he was just ignoring me, but he didn't respond. He just got into the chip truck, leaving me standing there all out of sorts.

After a few very pissed off moments of fuming, I turned and got back into the door of the warehouse. I had no idea who the hell the man was talking about; as far as I knew, I didn't have any kin out this way. I was spitting mad, and everyone gave me a pretty wide berth. A stack of boxes became my new home as I waited for something to happen.

As I sat and stewed, I watched a couple of men carry a few more crates out into the swamp. A bit later a man took a muzzled dog out the same direction. Clearly, I had settled down into Cock and Dog Fighting Central, or at least where they stored them till showtime. That just pissed me off even more. I felt like I was complicit. I mean, hell, I had helped bring some out here to die myself, thanks to my shit-heel daddy.

I was about of a mind to go do something about it and let off some real steam when a shit-brown Oldsmobile on busted shocks creaked and groaned its way into the back lot. A ruddy-faced young guy was behind the wheel, his strawberry-blond hair pulled back in a loose ponytail. He guided the big old car into an empty spot, then bounded out with far too much energy.

It suddenly occurred to me that all my drugs, save for maybe a half dozen pills and a small joint, were still in the fucking chip truck. In all my anger I'd totally forgotten, and that just set me right off even worse. I took to stomping and swearing up a blue streak.

After a moment I felt eyes on me, and I whirled. The red-faced guy was standing nearby, a huge grin on his face. He looked like he might burst into laughing at any moment. "What?" I snapped.

"Well, don't have to ask whose boy you are," the man said wryly. "Even if you didn't look about like his twin, you clear as shit got his temper."

That slowed me down, just a fraction. *This would be the cousin, then.* Looking him over, I didn't see much of a family resemblance, really. Marshes, we tended to be small and dark-headed, but this guy was close to six feet and kindly bright looking. Green eyes, reddish hair, pale skin but with a mess of freckles. And his clothes, jeans and a clean button-up, they fit in more with regular folks like my uncle Mike than the rank-and-file kin I was used to. He looked fucking lively. Healthy. It was damn near disgusting how . . . *vital* he looked.

"You'll be my cousin, then. Howard Marsh," I said, extending a hand. I didn't feel friendly and inviting, but if this guy was my ride, then I could play nice long enough to get myself into the car.

"Gralta Marsh. My name is Jack O'Connivan. Most folks call me Jackie-O, though."

"Jackie O'Convict, more like," said one of the workers there on the dock who happened to be passing by.

Jack doffed a pretend hat and grinned, twisting his hand into a middle-finger salute with a flourish. "Ignore the peasants, cousin. If you're done here, what say we hit the road?"

"Fine by me," I muttered, stalking toward the car, trying to figure out what I was gonna do with little money and even fewer drugs to get me through this weekend.

My cousin gave a little bow and gestured toward his ride. "*Krosh to de lorch!*"

The words made no sense, but they had a lilting quality to them that was real familiar. My eyes narrowed, but I decided to keep my mouth shut till I was inside the car. Then there would be some questions answered, I reckoned.

It's All Greek to Me

The interior of the car, at least, was a comfortable degree of trashy. A few fast food wrappers on the floorboard, a couple of crushed beer cans—the usual detritus that gave me that real homey feel. Even better, there was a half-empty sixer of PBR right by my feet.

Jackie-O slipped behind the wheel and pointed to the beers. "Help yourself. May even still be a bit cool from the station."

"Don't mind if I do," I said, pulling one from the plastic ring. It wasn't cold, but it wasn't warm, either, not that I would've much cared in my current state. It cracked open clean, and in one large swig I about half emptied it. I sighed and felt the anger sorta bleed out of me a bit. I was still mad, mostly at myself, but a few beers and a joint would probably have me in a good enough position to make it till I found some hard stuff.

"So, where we headed? Your da, he just told my da you was working for Frank on something. So, I got passed the job of playin' helper." The man didn't seem fazed by it. If anything, he seemed sort of happy.

I fished out the map from where I'd folded it up and slipped it into my pocket. "You know where Willy June had his wreck?" I asked, passing the paper over. "If not, Frank made a map. That's where I need to head. Not a huge rush, though. I need a little moonlight for what I got planned."

"I know the spot," Jack said, throwing the paper up on the dash. "That what you're caught up in, then? Frank reckon somethin' spooky going on there?"

I eyed him over. He went right to "spooky," so I guessed he knew enough about me. It was time to get some answers. "So, you're my cousin, huh? I didn't know I had any kin out this way. How are we related?"

"Pass me one of them beers and I'll tell ya," he said with a grin. It was dark enough that the headlights were on, lighting up the dirt road taking us away from Lagniappe. I noticed that one was fairly cockeyed, shining more up into the treetops than onto the road proper. I obliged the man and passed him one of the beers even as I watched the treetops. I was looking for a gap so I could judge the moon.

"Well, as I have been told, your grandma is my great-grandma's little sister." Jack belched. "They had some sort of falling out back when they was young, and your grandma ran off to marry your grandpa."

I'd had no idea that Granny was anything other than an only child. But then I hadn't exactly asked for details, and she wasn't the sharing sort. "Well, knowing Granny, that probably wasn't real pleasant."

That got a laugh out of him, but to be fair, he seemed like the kind of guy who laughed pretty easy. "So they say, so they say. Story goes that she took all the family's magic when she left. Which is crap, of course—it don't work like that. But it's true the O'Connivan haven't been flush with it since."

"Well, I don't know how flush our branch of the family is with it, but I reckon I got a chunk of it. Though shit all for training." I fished out my joint and lit it. I coughed a little, then breathed out a small cloud of smoke before offering it to Jack. He took it gratefully and toked as well.

Rolling down his window a crack, he puffed the smoke out with a couple of tight coughs. "Funny, that. I got trained up well enough—theory and all, I guess you could say—but I got barely enough power to light a fart."

I was instantly a bit jealous. Granted, knowing me, I would have squandered most any teaching I got, but it still would've been nice to have had the option. It felt surreal to be talking shop with someone outside of HD; I hadn't ever really gotten to do that before. Well, except a few times with Krista, but that hardly counted, seeing as how begrudging it was. Though she was getting a little better about that.

"Well, maybe you can show me trick or two," I said, taking the joint back. "But on a related note . . . seeing as you partake a bit, do you partake of anything a bit harder? In case I need a little juice, as it were."

Jack tapped his nose with one finger. "I can get you set up, no worries. But what do you mean, 'juice'?"

I shrugged. "I sorta . . . *supplement* my power, shall we say. A bit of this and that, and I can burn that energy to fuel whatever spell I'm working."

"Huh," he said, for the first time in a tone that wasn't all rays of sunshine and happy puppies. He didn't deign to say anything more, so I just left it at that. He could judge away; I hadn't a fuck to give.

We rode in silence for a couple of minutes. There was plenty enough moon for my spell, I could see now that we were out from under the trees. It was bright enough that the marshy land lining the road was sorta silver tinted, with ghostly reflections beaming up off the pools of water like quicksilver. It was quite a sight, to be honest.

"So, y'all live around here?" I asked finally.

Jacki-o snorted. "Only a few months a year. We're Travellers—didn't your da tell you?"

"Let's just say that the only way he tells me anything is if it directly benefits him. If not, he might as well be a fucking mute."

"I figured he'd have told you *something*, at least. Your gran, she turned her back on the family, but Tom made a point to reconnect. He speaks Shelta better than some of the young ones, in fact."

I eyed him. "Shelta . . . is that the gibberish you keep spouting at me?"

"Yeah. I'm guessing he didn't teach you any?"

"Can you learn it from the back of a hand? If not, then no," I snarked. "It's all Greek to me, I reckon." The joint was evening me out a bit. It was like each puff of smoke was gathering up some of my anger and releasing it out into the night air.

"Well, maybe I can teach you a bit of that, too." Jack grinned.

The man was being mighty helpful, and for no real reason I could see. I mean, sure, there was supposedly a bond of family, but I'd long ago learned that wasn't worth near as much as people tended to let on. He was angling for something, I reckoned, and I'd suss it out sooner or later. Till then, though, I was along for the ride—literally—as long as I kept out of my more paranoia-inducing delectables. Couple of those and I would get to the bottom of things . . . or just ruin them. Chances were fifty-fifty.

We'd been on the road about fifteen minutes when we came to a long straightaway, those cockeyed headlights shining off down the length and showing a whole lot of nothing. There were a few trees lining the road, but beyond them I got hints of what was probably some sort of field or pasture. It seemed like we'd reached a bit of dryer land, away from the marshes proper. There was moonlight enough to see a bit, but moving as we were, it was hard to tell.

Jack began to slow the car, though for no reason I could see. There was a curve up ahead but nothing too dramatic, and damn sure nothing that justified slowing to a stop. But stop we did, the car rolling to a halt in the knee-high grass on the side of the road.

"Willy June straightened this curve right out," Jack said, opening his car door. I followed suit and we both climbed out as he pointed in the direction the headlights were almost pointed at. "Hit that tree there."

I walked over, letting my eyes adjust. The drone of crickets filled my ears, keeping the clicking of the cooling engine company. I could detect the faint smell of singing grass from where it met the hot engine, crisping up nicely, no doubt.

There, on the very edge of the glow from the headlights, was a twisted tall tree. It looked like a cedar but it was hard to tell, seeing as all the leaves had been burned right off. The bark was gouged deeply, no doubt from the car, and most of what I could see left was just charred remains, black as the night around us.

My feet crunched on little bits of shattered safety glass as I neared, the last remnants of the wreck. As I got closer to the tree, I got a faint whiff of burnt wood with a hint beneath it that confirmed the charred mess before me was, in fact, a cedar. There was also a certain . . . *flavor* about it. I couldn't put it any better than that, but there was an echo of that swampy feeling I'd gotten back at the bar too.

"Do me a favor and cut off the headlights." For the first time, it really sank in just how lucky I'd gotten with my guide. Tom would have probably left me on the side of the road as soon as I started casting something, and with anyone else, I would've had to hide what I was doing.

"Going to commune with Gal Re?" Jackie-O asked as he reached through the open window to do as I asked.

"If 'Gal Re' means moon, then yeah, something like that."

The lights clicked off, and it was suddenly very dark.

Showtime.

Beyond the Black Horizon

Reaching down deep, I began to summon up my power. This wasn't my most powerful spell, but it was probably the coolest looking, and I felt like being impressive. I couldn't recall in recent memory having really impressed anyone, so why not try now?

I felt the power swirl and eddy within me, and drawing on its threads, I began to visualize the spell. I began to mutter a string of words, helping me shape the magic, control it. I didn't know what the words meant, but they were the words I knew, so I used them. If it ain't broke, don't fix it, as they say.

The video from earlier had given me a rough look at what Willy June had looked like, so that would help me focus. I pictured him and the time I knew the wreck had occurred, imagining what the scene would have been like. Visions of cars slamming into trees filled my head, and I let the power flow out of me and up to the moon.

Silver moonlight filled my vision, and I felt the spell catch hold of memory. Before me, I saw a spectral car materialize on the road. It couldn't tell what kind it was. It looked older—maybe some sort of Caddy or Pontiac. I didn't get much time to look, though, as it went roaring past me at incredible speed. It was clear that brakes were not in the picture.

The ghost of a memory slammed into the tree, crumpling like an accordion. The engine was pretty much instantly alight, it seemed, as I could see silver-blue flames go sparking up from the hood. I ignored that, though, instead focusing on the man inside the car.

I knew it was Willy June, but I'd never seen his face clearly, and it seemed I never would. He'd shattered out the glass of the windshield with his head and blood was pouring down his face, over his broken nose and smashed jaw. He was staggered, but somehow alive. Judging from how his chest was moving, the steering wheel had broken some, or all, of his ribs, and I had to imagine his lungs were Swiss-cheesed with bone fragments.

He was reaching for the door handle, which had me plumb amazed. How the man was still moving was a wonder—nightmarish, but a wonder nonetheless. I could see him wrench at the handle and saw the door give a little, as if it was stuck. Judging from the way frame was warped and crushed, it was no surprise the door wasn't working smoothly. June leaned back, turning so as to try and kick the door, it looked like. Then it happened.

From behind the man, a shimmery form appeared. A second later I could tell that it was the shape of a person, but spectral and not at all solid. It was more than just the effect of the spell; whoever this being was wasn't alive.

They had a broad face contorted in rage beneath a cleanly shaved head. Their skin, though silvery from the spell, was much darker in color than June's, and even through the spell their eyes glowed a fierce red. It was a gaze so hot, so angry, that I found myself stepping back. I knew I wanted no part of that.

That swamp smell was potent now, powerful, filling my nostrils as though I was submerged in the muck. I didn't know if it was the heat from the specter's eyes or from the flames (which, mind you, shouldn't be possible for either one), but it was suddenly getting mighty warm. I was dripping sweat, my heart was racing, and I felt fear tinging my spell. The silvery moonlight began shifting into a darker shade.

In the car, the spectral figure wrapped its arms around Willy June. You could see the man's face contort with pain as the pressure started crushing his shattered bones, and his mouth cracked wide in a silent scream. Behind him, the ghost just held on as the bigger man writhed and tried to fight back.

The ghost maintained its iron grip until the flames reached the cab of the car, then it faded away as June caught fire.

I stopped the spell, and the swamp smell began to fade. The shards of moonlight pooled onto the ground before they also vanished, taking the heat with them. I felt drained in a way I'd never felt with that spell before. I'd connected to something—something dangerous.

I just had to hope it didn't have my scent now.

"Well That Was Fuckin' Intense."

"**W**ell, that was fuckin' intense," Jack said, running a hand through his hair. "I know the spell, but I'd never seen it cast before. Never had the oomph. Kinda glad I haven't now."

"It's not normally like that," I said, shaking my head to try and clear my senses. "That was something . . . more. I think it got caught up in some sort of ghostly interference or something." I gave a little shudder. I could still feel echoes of whatever that had been: a ball of pure rage and swamp, an odd and impossible combination to describe. "Normally you see a little bit of silver outlines, then they vanish. This was more . . . well, everything, really."

"For what it's worth, I think I recognized the ghost thing," he offered. "He looked like Jamal, this guy who sometimes does odd jobs around town."

"This Jamal, he have power? Far as you know?"

"He ain't the brightest, really. A mule kicked him when he was little, they say, and he ain't been all there since. So maybe, but I'd be real incline' ta doubt it."

"Where's he live?" I asked, pretty sure the answer would be something along the lines of "He don't," judging from his ghostly presence.

Jack just shrugged. "I don't know. Probably down in the Quarters, if I had to guess. I mean, it's not like we were close or anythin'."

I was about to ask where that was, thinking about maybe heading out to try and find this guy, when my phone rang. The fact that I had signal at all was fairly surprising; I guessed they must have had antennas mounted to the cows 'round here. I saw it was Anna and answered. When I heard the drunkenness in her voice, I almost laughed.

"Howard. Marsh. You have abandoned me, but it is quite all right. I have found a new man, one who doesn't go off on adventures and leave me behind."

"Uh, excuse me?" I was too shocked to feel angry, but I knew that storm was coming.

"He's fat! And cute! And he might be drunk, too. I don't know, I think Krista gave him some of her beer."

I could hear Krista cackling in the background, which let me know there was some sort of joke afoot. It was a cackle I knew well—it was her "six beers in" laugh. It seemed like the girls had decided to hang out together without me, which I was sure I would come to regret for different reasons, but in the short term at least I could breathe a sigh of relief.

"Do you want to talk to him?" Anna giggled. I heard the phone being dropped, then picked up with a couple of faint curses in the background. Then I heard a wheezing noise that I instantly recognized.

"Hello, Horace," I said obligingly.

I heard the wheezing fade away, and then Anna's voice came back. "He said he loves me, and will never leave me! Are you jealous yet, Marsh?"

"Of you getting to curl up next to an ice-cream-sticky possum? Not particularly," I laughed. "Y'all at my shed, I take it?"

"Yep! I figured you would have forgot all about your baby, so Krista and I rode over to make sure he had food. And sure enough, I was right! His bowl was empty!" There was a lot of drunken judgment in her voice, but I just rolled my eyes.

"He had plenty for the weekend before I left! I made sure. Lardguts there just ate it all. He'd have been fine; he was gonna dumpster dive anyway."

"Marsh! He's your *child!*" The way she said "child," it came out as two syllables. *Chiii-eld.* "You can't let your child go hungry!"

I knew good and well that possum had been fat and happy long before I'd ever come into the picture, and since then he'd only gotten fatter. He was basically a butter tub on legs, and a sticky unwashed one, at that. Though I had no doubt that Anna had given him a bath since I'd left. The glee that critter got from my girlfriend soaping him up and rubbing him clean was damn near obscene.

"Babe, you know how much I like talking to you, but I'm sorta in the middle of something. You know how it is." I really did like talking to her, but I hated to be the sober guy in a conversation. If she was still up later, I might try her then, if I had a chance to get some more beer in me.

"No, it's fine. You've been replaced!" she said, and I heard her fumbling the phone for a bit as she grunted with effort. That wheezing, snuffling sound was back. "Horace is my new man, and he will love me forever!"

I laughed a little. I couldn't help it; she was a cute drunk. "Goodbye, babe."

"Tell Horace goodbye, too."

"Goodbye, Horace," I added. I swear the tone of his wheezing changed a little.

"Goodbye, Marsh," Anna said. Softer, she added, "I miss you."

"Miss you too, babe," I said, then I heard a click as the call disconnected.

I slipped my phone back into my pocket, wishing I was there with her instead of in fucking Mississippi. For a moment, I'd been able to drive the horror I had just seen from my mind, focusing on Anna. I was beginning to think I was falling in love with that woman. Hell, I might would even tell her that.

But then again, you gotta be careful. I like to set a low bar.

I looked over at Jack to see him grinning, no doubt from having overheard my end of the conversation. "How 'bout you stop grinning and start driving. Let's go find us a . . ." I still wasn't sure what we was hunting. "A Jamal," I settled on.

Jackie-O was already on his way back to the car. The game was afoot.

Change of Plans

Most anyplace in the South, you look around, you will find a place—usually on the shittiest, poorest land around—where there is a small community of Black people. The kind of land that white folks didn't feel motivated enough to steal back in the day or could've used to profit off of Black sweat. In Jubal County, there was Twelve Acre. In . . . uh, whatever county we were in, there was the Quarters.

Wealth travels down family lines. But when you start with basically nothing and the only thing you have to build upon is the poorest land in the county, well, then there ain't much to pass down. Families grow larger over time, and so a small pie keeps getting whittled down into ever smaller slices. Sure, some folks manage to get out, but they are the exception, I find.

And so you find yourself going down rough roads lined with small old shotgun houses. You can only keep something up so much before it gives slap out, and the houses in the Quarter were as close to giving out as possible while still standing. The streets were like my mouth: for every decent home you came across, there were twice as many rotting away. And, just like my teeth, it wasn't like there was any money to fix them. Though I have to imagine those homeowners didn't partake of illicit substances at the expense of . . . well, everything else quite the way I did.

Outside Grinwood this late, the few lights I saw were the scattered security lights lording over the clapboard ruins and run-down trailers. Turns out Jackie-O had no idea which house Jamal lived in, so we were more or less just cruising, looking for someone who was awake enough to ask. It wasn't the best plan, but fuck if I had one better.

After fifteen minutes of slow driving, Jack pulled into the paved lot of a small AME church. It was the first brick building I'd seen in a while, and you could tell someone was taking good care of the place. Folks in the South do dearly love them some religion.

"This is about the edge of things. Reckon we can turn 'round, give 'er another pass," Jack said, lighting a cigarette with a worn Zippo.

A flicker of movement had caught my eye, though, and I got out of the car without saying anything. I wasn't lubricated enough to be conversational at this point. I needed a lot more beer, and likely something *heavier*, to get my mind right. So instead, I ignored my chauffeur's shout of protest and walked over to the door of the church.

There was a sheet of paper there flapping in the night breeze, held to the bricks by a few bits of gray tape. It was a missing person's flyer. The face of a young Black man looked back at me, only this face was happy and smiling. When I had seen it just a bit ago, it had been twisted with palpable rage.

Jack came jogging up behind me and I pulled the flyer down and handed it to him. He looked at it, swearing under his breath. "Well, guess we found Jamal, then."

I swore too. "Yeah. Looks like we're dealing with a ghost after all." I looked back at the car, then at Jack. "Straight up, I am not high enough to deal with this shit right now. Change of plans: drugs first, then save the world or some shit."

Jack just shrugged. "End of the day, ain't my problem. So, whatever . . . I'm game to party a bit."

For the first time in a few hours, I smiled. "Fuck yeah."

Weekend Money

Turns out these Traveller folks were basically like nomads or something. Grinwood was only their home part of the year for most of them, a place to rest and relax a bit before they went out and about. Jackie-O wasn't real clear what it was they did whilst they was out of town, but reading between the lines, I got a feeling at least some of what they got into was on behalf of Frank.

Frank was a bit bigger fish than I'd reckoned if he had what was basically a whole damn village of folks doing shit on his behalf. And that's exactly what it was, though not any sort of group I'd ever spent much time in.

We were in the middle of a sort of big campground. There must have been a good thirty RVs in all different sizes. There were a couple of those big sorts, like what you see rich old folk trying to pull into gas stations too small for them. Most, though, were small and older-like, the kind you pull behind little tin cans with not much more than a bed inside.

It was late and only getting later, but there was a good bit of life in the Traveller camp. The two of us were kicked back in a couple of folding lawn chairs beneath an awning. The red-and-blue cloth spread out over us from a frame attached to Jackie-O's camper, a dark-blue bit of tin slightly more free of rust than most of the other small pull-behinds.

The heady, hyperactive glow of a fat rail of coke was running through me ninety to nothing, and I was starting to feel right. Beer in one hand, blunt in the other, and a pair of pills in my gut to complement it all, we watched the little bits of life we could see from our perches. Mostly it was men and women flitting from camper to camper, doing chores or something. Hell, I didn't know. For all I could tell, they were just a bunch of swingers going from place to place, banging up a storm. And I was blessedly far too high to care.

"I wish I knew where the fuck Jamal was," I thought out loud. If I'd known where his body was, I could've maybe done something about this killer ghost crap. "But I'm guessin' if the cops ain't got no clue, I'm probably not gonna do much better, being out of my element such as I am."

Jack snorted. "I don' know 'bout that. Don' think cops spend a lot of time huntin' for a missin' Black man, do you? Not exactly a high-priority case, if you catch my drift."

That carried a bit of weight, I reckoned. Jubal County wasn't too much different in that regard, though I'd like to think it might be a bit better. A *tiny* bit, though it pained my very fucking soul to give a cop any sort of credit. "Point taken. Still, though, unless you know some way Willy and Jamal were connected in some way, especially with Jerome and Kerrie, we got nothin'. Don't reckon Jamal played softball on a rival team or something, do you?"

"What's softball got to do with it?" Jack asked as he breathed out a cloud of smoke, then passed the blunt back.

"Frank was telling me his three boys, they played softball together. Maybe there was some sorta after-game squabble or something." I toked hard, which effectively shut me up.

"There ain't no softball teams around here. Where the fuck would they even play here in Grinwood?" Jack shook his head.

"Maybe they played out of town somewhere? Some place close by?" Had Frank lied to me? My gut said no, but then why the hell should I believe that? The man was a career criminal that hired my dad to do shit. Lying was like as not second nature.

"Maybe, but Willy June was sort of a homebody, Kellie was fat as hell, and I ain't never heard of Jamal leaving the area. He didn't have a car, just this little moped thing. Doubt he was driving it over to Meridian or some such. I'm not saying it ain't possible, but I got some serious doubts." Jack looked out into the darkness and barked a little shout—I'm guessing in Shelta, 'cause I didn't understand a damn word of it.

A broad figure came looming up out of the night. He looked about as much like Jack as I did my dad, close enough it was clear they were close kin. "Jackie boy," the other man said with a nod. He reached out a hand toward me, but his voice was guarded. "And you must be Black Tom's."

Before I could speak, Jack cut me off. "This here's Howard Marsh. Howard, this is my uncle Seamus. We were just talkin' about something, and I needed to know, Uncle, is there a softball team around here? One Willy June and a few other of Frank's boyos were playing on?"

Seamus snorted. "That what they tell you they was up to? *Softball?* Ain't no softball in Grinwood, you know that, boy. That there's code for what they were really up to."

"And just what might that be?" Jack asked, his eyes narrowing with thought.

Seamus made a motion over his head as though he was using his arms to make a triangle or a pyramid. "You know, men in pointy white hats who hang out together."

I felt my eyes widen. I knew the Klan was still around—I mean, I generally tried to ignore the news much as possible, but I wasn't totally oblivious. I'd just never heard of anyone actually being in it. Obviously *someone* had to, but to actually run into actual KKK members out in the world . . . it was almost surreal. "You're joking?" I asked, failing to keep the incredulity out of my voice.

Seamus cut me a puzzled look. "Why're you surprised? If Tom ain't worn a hood and gone on a night ride before, I'll eat my own shoes."

My stomach sank. That did sound right up my daddy's alley. I'd never really thought about it, I guess, because really? In this day and age? *The KKK*? What the fuck. I mean, I knew the South was backwards in a lot of ways, and I knew racism was alive and well. Seen it many, many times firsthand.

But the Klan? *What kind of idiot . . .*

Really, though, I should have known. The way ol' Tom acted, it made a whole lot of sense. He just knew better than to try and include me, I reckoned. Which, on the one hand, I was glad of, while on the other I was pissed I'd been so blind. I felt a real anger brewing up in me, and even though it didn't make any sense logistically, I decided then and there I'd be damned if I caught a ride back to Jubal County with the man.

Jack and his uncle were chatting away in that fancy language of theirs, leaving me out of it. I could've been offended, but I was working up too much of a cussing spell at my own closer kin. Besides, that meant that they weren't paying much attention to the blunt, which I did my best to put a hurtin' on. Call it a politeness tax.

The more I caught myself listening, the more I felt like I knew a word or two of their gibberish. Like, not quite that I knew the words, but that I knew words *like* the words. Like echoes, tiny little ghosts of the words bopping through the graveyard of their conversation.

It suddenly occurred to me that I was a good bit higher than I'd initially thought.

Hell yeah.

THE KLAN. REALLY. WTF. HOW DUMB DO YOU HAVE TO BE?

Once Seamus left, I believe I got onto a bit of a tear. I think if I'd known where a Klan meeting was going on, I would've tried busting up in there and slinging some spells around. I hadn't ever really cast spells at someone with the idea to hurt them, not unless they were also of a mind to hurt me, but damn it, some things you just can't stand for.

Luckily for all parties involved, Jackie boy sorta reigned my first impulses in. It's hard to talk sense into someone as high as me, but like some coked-up horse whisperer, he'd managed to keep me from galloping off. Not having keys was probably a helpful hurdle, I had to admit.

I was almost riled up enough that had Daddy actually been there, I might've would've said something. Of course, then he'd like as not have shot me, so again, that was probably for the best. But all this being foiled when I was riding high was really starting to get to me. I wanted to DO something right then and there.

"I wanna DO something!" I echoed my internal monologue out loud before I realized it. "Stick it to the man, as it were. Poke the hornet nest, stir shit up. Goddamn it, I want to find Jamal! And do another rail. And . . . fuck. Something! Anything!"

Jack just leaned back in his chair, which creaked a bit, the sun-bleached plastic threatening to finally give up the ghost. "Well, just how do you plan to find Jamal, then? What sorta leads you got?"

I got up and started pacing. Not pacing like someone professional—more of a lazy figure eight that involved a shit ton of arm waving. There may have been a few pointed jabs with my lit cigarette, putting periods on thoughts. It was much more involved than whatever some half-assed Sherlock would've pulled.

"We got a ghost of a missing Black man killing Klan members. I daresay we can put two and two together on that one, whatcha reckon? So, we either find the body and put it to rest, or we find anyone else involved in disappearing him and work it from that direction."

"That's fair. Got a plan to do that? I don't think too many folks are gonna openly claim they have a love of running around in white sheets on the weekend." He reached into a small cooler and pulled out a beer. "And I'm gonna hazard a guess that if folks knew where his body was, he wouldn't be considered missing anymore."

That was an issue. The thought I kept coming back to was that Frank had been the one to tell me his boys played softball together. Now, was that because they had told him that and he'd believed them? Or he was trying to divert me away from an uncomfortable secret—a secret that maybe the boss man was a part of? He seemed too smart to be so oblivious to the lack of a local softball team.

"Well, Frank, I reckon, knows who among his folks are in the Klan. Hell, he may even be one hisself."

At that, Jackie shook his head. "I don't doubt Frank knows who's who, but he hires a lot of Black folks, and I ain't never heard no call of him being racist. No more than your typical redneck Southerner, at least. He's always played us Pavees straight, and not many would do that."

"Well, he ain't playing things fully straight, and I don't know who else to talk to. Plus, I mean, if he knowingly hires Klan members, then he's racist. That's that. Really, I need to find the body and put it to rest. That's number one, but I ain't got any sort of connections here."

"Why not ask the Fair Folk? They could probably help you out."

I stopped pacing and turned to face Jack. "You mean like fairies and spirits and shit? Probably because I ain't never done so before. Is that an option?"

I knew Granny had trucked with spirits and the like, but I was under the impression she just sorta caught them and made them do what she wanted. Shoved them in a spell jar or some such and only brought them out as needed, like that Pooka I'd run into a while back. I just assumed that was the only way, and I hadn't a fucking clue how to really go about that. Spell jars were a closely guarded secret of hers.

Jack laughed. "God, you really don't know shit, do ya? I was thinking you was bullshitting me after I saw you speak to the moon, but I can see now that's not the case."

I began to bristle. A year or two ago I probably would've let that ride, as I kinda didn't care about how little I knew, but these days I was actually making a bit of an effort. Hell, I had even practiced my glyphs and such consistently in the past . . . well, probably month or so. Maybe month and a half. "Look now . . ."

Jack waved a hand. "I meant no offense. My uncle there, he knows more about the craft than anyone I've ever heard of—learned at his grandmother's feet. He can't cast much more than me, just a few tricks and such, but taught me as much as I could learn. Iff'n you're open to it, I'll show you what I know."

I closed my mouth. I was aching to tell him to fuck off, but that was just the pride talking. And even though I had far more pride than a toothless, jobless man such as myself should probably have, I knew I just needed to suck it up and take the help being offered me.

Even still, I decided I would get one over on ol' Jack before it was all said and done. *Can't have folks thinking they are better than me and such, family or no.* Preemptive, playful revenge, as it were.

That, or I would just do all his coke.

"We'll have to bribe them, though, to get them on our side. Scratch their back and they'll scratch ours, as it were," Jack was saying. "In the old days, they used bread and milk to make them happy, though these days you can tell them damn near anything is that and they'll believe you. But that just makes them listen to what you have to say. To get them to come up off some information, you got to give them something, or do something for them."

"What kind of shit do they want?" I knew basically nothing on this front, and even though it kinda chapped my ass to keep revealing how little I knew, there were bigger fish to fry.

Jack shrugged. "They like 'harmony in nature' shit. If they were more involved with humans these days, I think they'd be a bunch of eco-warrior types—save a forest, stop some hunters, that sort of shite. If you were a pretty young maiden, and a virgin, then some of the bigger fairy might take you for a ride, but seeing as you ain't—and we would probably be best keeping away from bigger forest spirit type shit—I don't reckon that's an option."

I thought of the King, flinching involuntarily. Yeah, bigger critters meant bigger problems, usually.

I got a sudden idea, one that scratched an itch that'd been bothering me damn near ever since I got involved in this trip. "Alright, let's see. What if we . . ."

It's a Bad Time, Bob

My hand was covered in blood.

The mosquitos had descended on me with a vengeance, and I spent about as much time slapping at them as I did walking. Though walking wasn't exactly easy, seeing as I found myself traipsing through a swamp, with all its viscous sucking mud.

To say that I was not a happy camper was a woeful understatement. My head was pounding with the blunt trauma of a hangover, and I was feeling like ass to an exceptional degree from coming down from my drug cocktail the night before. My head hurt, my eyes hurt, my tongue felt swollen, and I just sorta wanted to die.

I'd puked up the shot of whiskey Jackie had given me upon waking. *Hair of the dog, my ass.* Since then, about every fifteen minutes, as regular as clockwork, I hurled some more. There was so little inside me at this point that I was just dry heaving with perhaps just a little bile and blood for spice. The blood was from my throat, which was so ripped up from puking that I could barely talk.

Not that I wanted to, except for cursing.

Jack had taken us down a twisting maze of muddy roads, circling us back around till we was somewhere sorta near Lagniappe, but coming at it from a different angle. He claimed we'd planned all this out the night before, but fuck if I could remember. I mean, I knew that I had come up with something I'd believed to be brilliant at the time, and we'd agreed it was a great idea . . . but I could only remember just the very broadest strokes. I hadn't had it in me to argue, though, and now that I was up to my ankles in mud about every fourth step, I was really starting to regret that fact.

I hoped that the lingering drugs in my system were poisoning the fuck out of the legion of bugs trying to feast on me. I hoped they got a taste, tripped balls, and collided into a tree or something. Or better, that they got eaten by a bird that, in turn, started tripping and slammed into a tree. The fucking birds would not shut the fuck up, and every little tweet was basically a dagger in my brain.

Jack had been nice enough to stop walking long enough for me to crush up my last two pills and give them a quick snort. I just had to hope that I wouldn't snot it out the next time I hurled. It didn't make me feel better much, at least not overall, but at least I didn't have that all-too-familiar itch adding to my list of complaints. Of course, I then learned that lecturing was seemingly in our blood as Jack did his best impression of HD, droning on about the dangers of heavy drug use. *Like you didn't go line for line with me last night.*

Of course, he hadn't mixed it with quite the host of other substances that I did. And he was also real fucking chipper, which made me want to kill him. Maybe a tripping bird would shit on his head or something.

All things considered, I thought I was holding it together pretty well. I wanted to die, but I was keeping it to myself, not burdening the world with it. Sure, I'd had a bit of a shit fit about a half dozen mosquito slaps back, but that had only lasted maybe a minute. I'd barely even shouted all that much.

My shoe came off in the mud. One minute my foot was safely encased against the intruding muck, and the next I found myself taking a step forward with one socked foot. Not before I'd stutter-stepped and sunk that foot straight into six inches of musty, opaque swamp water, of course. I froze, my mind going blank in an explosion of white-hot rage. I was about to scream out my anger—and probably whip up a spell to burn down this whole fucking swamp, and then hopefully the world at large—when a hand quickly clamped over my mouth.

I was so caught by surprise that I actually fell backwards, going ass-first into the mire and filth, and had the rage shocked right out of me. I was so far beyond anger at that point that I could not function. My eyes just stared ahead, locking on to Jack as I contemplated the quickest way to kill him. If my head hadn't been pounding so hard, I probably could've even done it.

"Hey, quiet now," he whispered. "We're basically there."

I think my mouth was kinda working—fish flopping, as it were—as I tried to come up with some sort of world-ending curse or even just a pithy retort. However, I failed. All I really managed to accomplish was letting my ass get progressively wetter as I slowly sunk down into the swampy sludge.

Jack extended a hand, pulling me to my feet. I hopped there awkwardly on one foot as I guided my sodden sock-covered toes toward the mudhole enclosing my other shoe. A few moments of wrangling, a couple of soft curses, and one more near tip back into the muck later, I was back on my shit-kickers, ready to handle business.

Through the trees and brush I could see the faint outline of a building. The standard swamp sounds filled my ears, trickling water and loud-ass frogs and the like, but I could also hear the occasional bark of a dog or rooster crow. This had to be where Frank and the crew hosted their weekly dog and cock fights.

Jack had a Walmart bag in one hand, passing it to me. "Just like we talked about, alright?"

I took the bag and looked inside blankly. There was a red Solo cup, a Moon Pie, and a glass bottle of Highlife. "Let's pretend I was real high when we talked about this plan and that perhaps the finer details have escaped me."

Jack snorted, but kept his smile. *Chipper fuck.*

"Set the cup on the ground, pour in the beer, and unwrap the Moon Pie and set it on the ground beside it. Then I'll tell you what to say."

I did as he asked, ruining a perfectly good Moon Pie, much to my chagrin, though the thought of eating it made my stomach send off a warning rumble or two. The Solo cup, I sorta sunk into the mud a bit so it wouldn't tip, then poured out the yellow-gold beer in. I had to hold my breath as I did it, fairly certain the beer stink would send me hurling again.

Straightening up, I took a step back. Jack motioned to a nearby log that was marginally dryer than the surrounding area, not that my soaked ass would much notice, and we both sat. "Repeat after me, and think thoughts about summoning up fey folk."

I had no idea what kind of thoughts those would be, but I just went with it. He said a string of gibberish words that tickled the back of my mind. "Those sound sorta familiar," I said.

Jack rolled his eyes. "How long is it gonna take you to realize the spell words you know are Shelta? Your grandma, she spells in Shelta, same as us. The meaning don't matter, just the intent—that's why you can use them."

I was pretty sure he'd added "idiot" onto the end of that, but I graciously chose to ignore that. Instead, I just asked him to repeat the words and I began to mangle my way through them as best I could. Managing to not throw up while doing so was the real magic.

I started trying to "think fey thoughts." I took that to mean imagining the little critters coming up out the swamp and hanging around the offered snacks. Most folks can't see fey, or rather if they do, I think they just immediately forget that they have. You have to have at least a little magic in you to see them head-on. They are sneaky and rare, though, hard to spot unless you really go hunting them. At least, that's been my experience on the few times I've toked up and gone "snipe hunting."

As I worked my jaw around the unfamiliar words, Jack whispered to me, "This spell, it sorta thins things out. We should start seeing things the way the fairies do in a bit. That will make it easier to see, if it shows."

Even as he was talking, the colors of the world became a bit more . . . bright. Dark greens became light greens and light greens became neon, damn near glowing. The brown muck started to look richer, and the little bits of sky I could see were a piercing blue all of a sudden. It was like looking at the world through super sunglasses or something, making everything look that much more alive.

I had faith this would work after all, especially with all the Lite-Brite shit going on, but it was still a butt-puckering surprise when the fairy actually came up out of the undergrowth. I had only been repeating myself for maybe two or three minutes, and I hadn't even really been saying the words all that accurately toward the end there. I was half-assing in the extreme, yet there it was.

Every fairy I'd ever seen had looked real different from each other. Not sure why, but this one certainly fit that bill. It was maybe the size of my hand with skin that was fairly green in color. It had a decent little potbelly, betraying a steady diet of junk food and beer, and you could tell it was magic just by how tiny its wings were in comparison to its bulk.

The wings themselves were not the gossamer things you saw on Tinker Bell. These looked like a moth had fucked an oak leaf and had a weird little wing baby. Coupled with the green skin and the artfully worn acorn hat codpiece, you could damn near smell the nature coming up off this thing. There were even a few strands of Spanish moss that served as the critter's hair, flowing back in the breeze from between a pair of horns.

Tubby beelined for the Moon Pie, which, to be fair, I would likely have done as well. This wasn't some trash-ass vanilla Moon Pie—no, this was the full chocolate big boy. It was almost as large as the fairy itself, but that didn't slow it down none. It dove face-first onto the pie, pulling handfuls of snack-cake goodness free to cram into its surprisingly large mouth.

Jack waved for me to stop repeating the words and we rose to our feet, walking softly toward the creature. It paid us no attention, no doubt thinking we couldn't see it. Or maybe it was just too caught up in stuffing its face.

We stood there silently, looming over it, bathing it in our shadows. After maybe ten or twelve seconds it finally looked up, crumbs covering its face and chest. It looked from one of our faces to the other, back and forth a few times, and you could see the realization slowly crest over its face.

"You can see me, can't ya?" it asked finally. I had expected its voice to be thin and high-pitched, like some sort of squeaky helium voice, but instead it sounded perfectly normal, as if it had come from a normal-sized person. I didn't have to struggle one bit to hear it. I nodded.

"Aye," said Jack. "We're who left you the gifts there."

The fairy reached down blindly, never taking its eyes off of us, and snagged another handful of Moon Pie. He raised it to his mouth, taking a too-large bite, but somehow managing to swallow it down. "Thnks," it mumbled through the crumbs.

"I need a little help," I said, keeping my voice soft.

"Ooo, hard no," the little critter said before dunking his head into the Solo cup to slurp down some beer. "Thanks for this, though. Much appreciated."

"It's a simple thing, though, just a snippet of information."

"I'm flattered you think I know what you need, really, but how about you just let me eat and drink in peace, and I don't curse you?"

Jack cut in. "What if we did you a big favor?"

The fairy arched a tiny eyebrow. "Doubtful, but I'm listening. But only because this is some *damn* good milk and bread."

"So here's what we were thinking . . ."

Barking Up the Right Tree

We hunched low, watching the outbuilding for any signs of life. We knew that inside there were dogs and such, but was there somebody in there feeding them? Tending them? That was the question.

Unlike the fancy new warehouse that had been built onto the back of Lagniappe, or even the old but fairly well-cared-for bar itself, this building was nothing but a hunk of junk. It had clearly been a barn at one point, though just what it would have held was beyond me. Not a lot of farming one can do in a swamp.

It was sure enough big, though, even if you could see where along the base of the building where repeated flooding had rotted the boards. Above the waterline it was a weathered brownish gray, blending in fairly well with the trees covered in Spanish moss that filled the surrounding area. You could see where there had been windows once, but the glass was long gone, busted out over the years by God knows what.

The front of it had a big barn-type door, large enough to drive a tractor into, but that was not where we were angling for. No, we were staking out this little side door, just a normal people-sized number that looked a little newer than the rest of the place. It looked like it got a good bit more use, so we'd figured if anyone was heading in or out, that would be the place.

I was feeling somewhat better now. I didn't think I had anything left in me to puke anymore, and my hangover was fading just a little bit. Getting to just sit in one place, and in the shade, that was helping, too. It made it easier for the mosquitos to get me, but at this point I would happily swap a little bloodletting for a decent break.

"I don't think anyone's in there," Jack said for the third time. I was firmly in agreement, but I also wasn't feeling real motivated to get moving. I could've gone for a nap—and then some nice hard drugs—but I figured I'd settle for being lazy just a bit longer. "Let's go."

Jack didn't wait for me to respond; he just set off at a quick trot, keeping his body low to the ground. I swore but dutifully followed after, my muscles protesting with every step and begging me to sit my ass back down. Struggling as I was, I still managed to fight down that impulse and kept up with my cousin.

He reached the door first, scuttling up and placing an ear against it. If he heard anything, he must have not thought it too important, because a few moments later he opened the door and ducked inside. With a sigh, I followed, crossing my fingers that we weren't about to get caught fucking with my potential new benefactor. Now, I sure as hell didn't mind that were about to fuck over Frank; I just didn't want to get caught at it until I got paid.

Someone at some point had strung lights in the barn, but they were all off just then. That didn't matter much, though, as sunlight was streaming in through the open windows as well as the cracks in the boards. It wasn't all that bright in there, but it was easily light enough to see.

The smell was what I noticed first. The air was heavy with the stink of dog and chicken shit, a thick animal smell. It was the stench of captivity, and it caused my stomach to churn. I could tell that no one had given the place a decent cleaning recently, and coupled with the heat, the funk was almost overpowering.

The dogs spotted us pretty much instantly, and when one started barking, they all did. Inside the confines of that barn it was painfully loud, and I knew that if we didn't do something quick, someone was bound to notice. At least the roosters were staying somewhat quiet, no doubt cowed by the howling.

A half dozen dogs, mostly pit bulls but also one heavily scarred-looking German shepherd, were being kept in separate chain-link kennels. Jack was already moving to the first and I just watched, standing by the still-open doorway. Taking a second, I quickly glanced out the door and up the hill toward Lagniappe. *So far, so good.*

Something about Jack sure calmed them pups down. As soon as he got close, they went from snarling killers to happy tail-wagging puppies, damn near. Far as I could tell, he wasn't doing anything fancy, just muttering the usual shit like "Who's a good boy?" As he popped open those kennel doors, they took to bouncing up, jumping all over him till he pretty quickly had a swarm of happy dogs around his feet.

Grinning bigger than I'd ever seen, which was quite a feat, he then went strolling past me and out the door. The dogs just followed, happy as you please. "You're on rooster duty," he laughed over his shoulder, using his arms to play with his new entourage.

I looked up the hill one last time and, seeing no one, scuttled over to where the roosters were crated up. Besides the six I had helped Daddy bring, there were three others, all still in their cages. A quick glance showed me that they didn't have the lethal spurs on—I guessed they got put on right before a fight, maybe—so I just started opening up the cage doors.

In my head, I figured that whatever fairy magic Jack had used to wrangle them dogs would surely work for me too. Granted, I was just assuming there *was* fairy magic; the idea that maybe he was just one of those dog people, or had a certain knack like Uncle HD, never really crossed my mind. I would open the doors and those roosters would just follow right along like I was the pied piper of cocks, I reckoned.

That was patently not the case.

The first rooster just sorta hung around. The second didn't want to come out the cage. When I finally got it out, that caused the first rooster to go scurrying off, then the third rooster getting added to the mix meant that all three started flapping around like mad. Number four got into a fight with number two, and I got my face scratched the fuck up separating them. By that point three had run out the door, and one was up in the fucking rafters.

By ignoring all the chaos erupting around me, I somehow managed to get all nine crates open. That turned out to be the easy part—now I had what looked to be like seven roosters running around like they didn't have their heads on, going gangbusters around the inside of the barn. I had to guess that two had already escaped, and I was sorely tempted to just say fuck it and leave every chicken for themselves.

Instead, I took to chasing chickens. I would catch one, get pretty good and scratched up, and then go running for the door. I hurled those fuckers with a vengeance, launching them out the door with all the rage I had in my body. They, of course, just flapped their wings and landed a few feet away. The whole thing was so ineffective that it just kept making me more and more mad.

If I hadn't been doing this to save the little bastards' lives, I would've just killed them, and done it with a mad gleam in my eye and a smile on my lips. Instead, I managed to get all but one out of the barn, my arms and face oozing a disturbing amount of blood. I had also managed to throw up a few more times yet, and I could smell my sweat on my body. It reeked of booze, which only made me even more sick.

The last rooster was still up in the rafters. I spent about five minutes trying to coax that little fucker down and tried to think of a spell that would help, but nothing came to mind. The bastard just sat up there clucking away, watching me. I *swear* it was watching me—just staring at me smugly with those beady little rooster eyes. It was gloating. I know it.

In the end, I gave up. I figured you probably couldn't have a cock fight with just one rooster, so it would like as not be safe enough in the short term. Maybe it would even make its own escape once I left. I couldn't be bothered anymore, and time was limited. Who knew when someone might come down?

I was walking out the door when something landed on my shoulder, causing me to shriek and freak slam the fuck out. That one fucking rooster just held on for dear life, digging its claws into my shoulder as I thrashed around sure as shit that some kind of monster had gotten me.

By the time I calmed down, the thing had made itself right at home. I tried getting it to turn loose, but it straight up wasn't having it. That was a hurdle for another mo-ment—a moment *far* away from men with guns—so I just decided to let it ride and looked around for the rest of the roosters.

They were all gone. There were a couple of feathers on the ground, likely resulting from my angry tosses, but other than that? Not a single fucking bird in sight. I'm maybe not the most observant person in the world, but eight black-and-white roosters running around, even I could spot.

Fuck it. I started to head off toward where Jack and I were supposed to meet up, winged asshole in tow.

But then I thought about why we'd done what we just did. About how they would like as not just scrounge up some more dogs and roosters for next week, or the week after. We'd given them a little speed bump, but it wouldn't really hurt them any.

With a wicked grin, I called up a little ball of fire. Taking a quick glance to make sure no one was around—which I probably should have done before summoning fire from the air, I admit—I hurled my fist forward. The ball arced into the air, flying through an open window to smack against the roof. I watched a moment to make sure it caught good, then tore the fuck out of there.

CAIN ENABLER

When I caught up to Jack, I saw the dogs were all gone as well. I didn't ask what happened; I was too out of breath. That rooster was still clinging to my shoulder, and if I wasn't sure that the fucker would rip out a hunk of flesh as it went, I would have smacked the damn thing off me. Luckily, Jack was able to coax it down to the ground, even if he was an annoying little shit that giggled the whole damn time.

We sat down to wait again, back on the same log we'd copped a squat on earlier. Jack was whistling a little tune while I kept an eye on the rooster. I *swear* it was eyeing me back. We just kept cutting wary glances at each other, making no sudden moves.

Jack noticed the smoke before I did. I had, uh . . . neglected to alert him to my last-minute addition to the plan. He stood up suddenly, looking back toward the barn. You could just barely see the orange flames through the thick woods, and a column of smoke was rising up through the trees. "You have something to do with that?" he hissed.

"Yep."

"Where you gonna tell me?" he asked angrily, the ever-present grin slipping from his face.

I just shrugged. "Needed doing."

Jack huffed, then sorta stalked around the clearing for a bit. He kept his eyes on the fire, fretting up a storm. I reckoned it was probably too wet to spread, so it seemed to me he was fussing over nothing. When I began to hear distant shouting, though, I reckoned that maybe I should have at least waited till we could chill someplace a little farther away. The yells, no matter how distant, did succeed in getting Jackie-O to sit back down, I supposed trying his best to stay out of sight. I thought the odds of anyone seeing us through all them trees, especially when there was a big-ass fire going, wasn't too likely, but whatever.

Jack had just produced a joint and fired it up when our fairy buddy made his appearance once more—only this time, instead of flying up into the little clearing, he came in riding on a rooster. Where he'd managed to find a tiny chicken-sized saddle, I hadn't a fucking clue, but he rode in like he owned the damn place.

That rooster was high-steppin', let me tell you. And when it caught sight of "my" rooster, it sorta puffed up like it was trying to look even more important, which kindly pissed me off. It shouldn't have—I hated that fucking thing—but to a degree it had chosen me, I reckoned, so I'd be damned if some fairy mount made my cock feel inferior.

"Your offering is suitable," the little fey thing said. "You've saved many lives, and done us a great service."

"So you'll tell me where to find Jamal?" I asked.

The fairy waved its hand in a broad, sweeping motion, then turned and rode away. The rooster was gettin' it as it tore away from the clearing. I'd never seen one move that fast, but then I felt safe in assuming magic was at work.

"Rude little prick didn't even tell us!" Jack said, his mouth open in disgust.

"No, it did." I could feel the tug on my soul, pulling me in the direction we needed to go. "Follow me."

It ended up being a pretty long walk. Several miles, enough distance that while we were a decent distance from Lagniappe, we weren't really all that far from the road. It was still swamp, and thus unpleasant to be in, but I was starting to be able to see the beauty of it as my hangover faded.

The little bit of drugs I'd managed to bum off Jackie-O helped as well. Half that joint, along with the last of my pills powdered and snorted, made for a much happier Marsh. I could've done with some more—read: a lot more—but we all have our crosses to bear.

I knew I was heading for trouble if I didn't track down a sizable amount of heavy stuff, and soon. Addictions are a bitch like that. The little bits I'd been able to score had just sorta kept me going, but not exactly flourishing, as it were. But that was a problem for later.

The issue now was that I had very little drugs in my system, at least compared to the cocktail I usually managed to muster up in my blood. The kind of hodgepodge of poisons that I could easily draw on to fuel my magic. We were about to go find us a ghost, and while I hoped that it would go pretty smooth, if it didn't . . . well, let's say I had very little to draw on.

"I think we're getting close," I said. The tugging was getting stronger with each step.

"Alright, then. He gonna be beside the road, you think?" Jack asked, pointing before us. You could see the paved road up ahead, maybe a hundred yards off.

I shook my head. "The way I figure it, every time I touch on this ghost, I get a smell of swamp. Jamal's gotta be buried in the muck. Hopefully not too deep, seeing as we ain't got a shovel."

"We can always go back and get one. So, what are we thinking happened? Jamal got hit by a car, driven by these guys?"

I moved a branch out of the way, holding it so Jack could pass through. "I think he was at Lagniappe, or at least real close by, when these fuck-wits did whatever they did. Maybe they hit him with a car, but I doubt that. No, he was at Lagniappe, at least at some point."

"Why's that?"

"That slot machine. Jamal's got a lot of anger, but most ghosts, even real angry ones, they can't really fuck with us. Not for real. Poltergeist shit, maybe, but wrecking a car like that? Nah. I think he used that slot machine to trick himself inside these fucks and possess them." I remembered the sight of Willy June taking some money from the slot machine and folding it into his wallet. "I think the money they won out that slot machine was a sliver of Jamal. And when they took it, he worked his way into their heads, and then . . ."

"And then? What, made them kill themselves?"

"We're here" was all I said.

I'd seen this exact sight when I first touched the echo of the ghost back at Lagniappe. A huge cypress tree, one of the biggest I had ever seen, growing up from a low mound, Spanish moss so thick on the damn thing that you could hardly see anything more than ten feet off the ground, almost like a gray wall.

"Fuck," Jack said in a low voice, pointing toward the base of the tree.

There, jutting up from the muck, was a skeletal hand.

I didn't realize how much I'd locked in on those bones until I heard Jack throwing up behind me. I was fixated, unable to tear my eyes away. They filled my vision, and the longer I looked, the more empty and hollow I felt inside.

Something had chewed the meat right off those bones. Only a couple fingers were still attached, and dotting the ground around it were small white bits of bone. I could see where something had tried digging down, trying to get to more of the corpse, but hadn't yet finished the job. There was a sour, sick odor in the air, the scent of decay.

I finally tore my eyes away, taking long, deep breaths as I fought back the urge to be sick yet again. Everyone's seen a dead body before, but there is a gulf of difference between seeing your great aunt all done up in a coffin and coming up on a poor dead guy with his hand chewed off. I was shook, no two ways about it. I looked up, trying to focus anywhere but on that body. And that's when I saw it.

Hanging from a limb, almost blending in with all the moss, was a noose.

Jack was wiping his mouth, pointedly turning his back on the macabre scene. "So what, then, we call the cops? Get Jamal proper buried so he'll rest easy?"

"Something like that. That comes later, though. For now . . ."

I scooped up a finger's worth of muddy soil, rubbing it slowly between my fingertips. It was wet, a little cool to the touch. Like as not it was staining my fingers brown, but that was a distant concern. Instead I focused on that feeling I'd had back at the bar, repeating the same words, trying to rebuild that faint connection.

Something slammed into me, and everything went black.

Mourning of the Earth

Out of the darkness came the sound of heavy boots crunching on the ground. Thick, drunken laughter, like the braying of mules, filled my ears. Fear gripped my heart. I felt pain in my face, my ribs. I was struggling to breathe.

When light came, it was from headlights. They burned my eyes, and I tried to raise an arm to shield my face, but a heavy boot knocked it wide. I felt bone snap and cried out, sobbing against the pain.

Legs, too many to count easily, surrounded me. They were outlined against the blare of the truck's headlamps, a circle of thick leather boots and hard worn jeans. *Why are they doing this? What did I do to deserve this?*

Boots and spit rained down on me and I doubled over, clutching a broken arm against broken ribs. I tried to yell, but all that got me was a thick fist brought down on my jaw. It might have broken. I couldn't tell. It hurt, bad, but it was just one lightning crack of pain amongst many.

The laughter, though. *Why? Why are they laughing?*

A shriek. Not mine—I couldn't have shrieked if I wanted to. Moaning was all I could muster, and that just brought on more pain.

A voice, different from the four laughing men. One I thought I knew, female, angry, loud. Shouting at the men to stop, to leave him alone. I hoped "him" meant me, and that they listened. The blows stopped for a moment, and I got a sense of men shifting to block the sight of me.

"Get back in the fucking bar. This don't concern you!" came a yell. I knew that voice—he'd been the one to start all this. To start the fight. To break my ribs.

I heard a loud crack, then a scream. The woman wasn't trying to save me anymore, but the blows had stopped coming. Thick hands pawed at me instead, picking me up. Cool metal crashed against broken bones and skin as they threw me into the bed of a truck. I think someone was in the back with me, but mostly I just heard laughter as men piled into the cab.

I wanted to sleep. To be left alone. But it all hurt—it hurt so bad. I kept crying, just bawling like a baby. I asked why they were doing this, why they were hurting me. What had I done?

"Shut up!" came a shout. I felt something wet on my face. It trickled into my mouth, sour and musty. Beer, like the kind my older brothers would sometimes steal from our granddaddy's fridge. I sputtered, trying to spit it out. I was sure a thick wad of blood went with it.

That spit must have gone where it shouldn't have, because then something came crashing down on my head. Everything went real dark.

The darkness faded again, but I didn't know how much time had passed. I wasn't in the truck bed anymore; I was propped up between two men, their arms holding me up. My wrists were tied behind him, so tight I could hardly feel them anymore. Though if I could have felt it at all over the pain in my shattered arm, I didn't know.

My head, which had been lolling against my chest, I managed to lift a little. One eye was swollen shut, but the other could see the little clearing I was in. Silvery moonlight swamp was all around, but mostly I was focused on the man standing across from me. He was leaned on a shovel, holding a flashlight in one hand. The beam was pointed up over my head.

"Please, just lemme go," I sobbed.

That's when the rope passed over my head, and someone behind me pulled it tight. I was lifted into the air, my legs flailing as I tried to break free.

Halo Slipping Down

"**J**aysus, Marsh!"

My eyes flashed open. I was rising into the air, being lifted by something around my throat. My hands leapt to my neck fast, finding their way to the rope that had encircled it. The rough material scratched at my skin, and as I frantically tried to dig my fingers between the rope and my flesh, I felt my nails scratching red lines into my neck.

I realized I was gasping for air, but the rope was far too tight. My eyes felt like they were bulging right out of their sockets as I struggled to free myself. All I could see were the limbs above me growing closer as I rose up, the gray moss seeming to reach for me.

Rough hands gripped my ankles as I felt Jack trying to tug me down. All that managed to do was slow my ascent slightly while also causing the rope to dig ever tighter into my throat. I needed a knife or something, but I had nothing, and the rope was too tight for me slip my finger in to give myself some breathing room. My vision was starting to fade around the edges, a shadow of darkness that signaled my impending doom.

I could've easily burned through the rope if I'd been able to make a sound. I'd never cast a spell without words before, and I wasn't exactly in the mindset to try and suss out how in just that moment. Instead I started trying to reach for the knot, hoping I could work it loose before I died.

Jack jumped up and wrapped his arms around my waist. My neck cracked painfully, and for a moment I thought the damn fool had broken it. He hadn't, but I bet I gained a good three inches in height all of a sudden. That quickly became a secondary concern, however, as above me I heard the limb begin to crack and groan.

With a loud snap, it broke, a wrenching crack of wood giving way under our combined weight. It came free and I landed on top of Jack with a thud, and a heartbeat later the limb crashed down on top of me. The pain of the impact knocked me under, then dragged me right back up out of unconsciousness. I'd have cried out if the rope hadn't still been knotted tight around my throat.

Jack rolled out from under me and thankfully set to work on the noose. Within a few seconds that felt more like hours, he had the rope loose enough that I was able to start gasping for breath. Each shuddered gasp hurt like hell, but my angry lungs slowly began to work once more. I could feel the wet ground beneath me, but for once I didn't care. I hurt in far too many places in that moment to give a rat's ass about much of anything.

My throat was on fire, and my back felt like someone had taken a bat to it. The damn limb was lying across part of me, but I had zero gumption to try and move it. I just wanted to lay there and preferably die quickly rather than drag it out like I had been doing. At least then the pain would stop.

Jackie-O was freaking out, of course, chattering up a storm, but I was too busy trying to will myself dead to listen. I knew I've been doing something, anything, really, but damned if it wasn't all just a bit too much at that moment. I suddenly felt a bit silly for trying so hard to live just a few moments ago. That's what I got for not thinking ahead, as always.

In spite of my pity party, I could feel Jamal trying to gather up enough power to launch some other sort of attack. I wasn't worried, though. If the guy could work big magic quickly, all them fucks who'd killed him would've been found dead in a night, not over the course of several days.

Granted, this close to his body he could probably lash out a little quicker, but I still had time.

Jackie-O was still just muttering away. He lifted the limb off me and was patting me down, feeling for broken bones. At least I hoped that's what he was doing—a couple of those pats touched on places a bit close to home, if you catch my drift. All in all I just wished he would quiet the fuck down and leave me alone. I hurt, and would continue to hurt, but honestly that's more or less how I lived my life most times anyway. I had learned how to deal.

"Jack," I managed to rasp out. That one word hurt like a punch to the throat.

"Marsh, thank God! What, man? What can I do?"

"Shut up," I forced out. He'd managed to annoy me to the point of rousing me from my moment of weakness.

I staggered to my feet. I had landed mighty close to Jamal's outstretched hand, and I jumped back as soon as I realized that. There was a latent anger to the air, like the electricity before a storm, and I could feel it slowly building. Stomping on his corpse wouldn't help matters, I was sure.

"He's killed three of the four what did this to him," I managed to croak out. I needed some cold water to soothe my throat, but all there was around was swamp water.

Seeing as I didn't fancy a case of cholera, I knew I would just have to let it pass.

"Are we safe?" Jack asked, his eyes locked onto the rope.

I nodded. "For a couple hours."

"Who's the fourth?" he asked. "Anyone you know?"

I thought back to the vision I'd just lived through. It had been like looking through fogged-up glasses, so not a lot was clear and the memory was fading fairly fast, at that, but there had been two voices I knew. One was the girl from the bar, the bartender I'd talked to earlier. The other, the one I now knew had given her that shiner—and not the beer—was Black Tom.

"Yep. Unfortunately."

THE FINAL TALLY

I was sitting across the desk from Frank, watching his face. He had a good poker face, that was for sure, so it was impossible to tell what it was he'd already known.

"So, we put a pile of sand near Jamal's grave. White sand, the kind that'll stand out like a sore thumb to any cops who investigate, but we didn't have a choice. Jamal will be compelled to count that sand, grain by grain, until he gets it all. It'll buy you enough time to figure out how you want to get this reported."

Frank frowned. "Why would I want to report a murder that took place at my bar? A hate crime, no less, done by my own employees. This is Mississippi, but come on. And I doubt you're going to want me to turn in your own father."

"You'd be wrong there, in fact. Fuck Tom. Nothing would please me more than to see him go to prison. But here's my trouble: If he finds out I reported him, he'll kill me. Hell, I think if he'd realized what he was bringing me in on, he'd have probably just killed me on the way here. He has a very scorched-earth approach to folks who have wronged him, both in actuality or potentiality.

"But there's two other factors in play here. First, Jamal can't touch Daddy. Don't ask why—it's just the way of things. He's a dead zone, as it were, no pun intended. And if Jamal can't go after the guy who actually killed him, he's like as not going to get real angry, and that sort of angry leads to some real bad shit. Think *Amityville Horror* meets *Candyman.* You need to get him buried in consecrated ground, and fast. You do that, and this should all go away."

"What's the other factor?"

"Besides it being the right thing to do, you mean?"

Frank's frown deepened. "Right."

"Well, you got a bartender here who I think may know what happened, or who at least suspects. They tried to stop it from going down, even. They've kept quiet this long; they may keep on. But they may not, if the guilt keeps eating at them. I suspect you'd rather control the narrative, as it were, and I don't want this bartender suffering bad shit at the hands of my daddy. So, you should call it in. I don't care how you square it, so long as Jamal gets buried and justice gets served. Daddy will go to ground, no doubt, and good luck catching him, but

I want it to get out that these three dead guys and him were responsible."

He sat there in silence for a time, his eyes just steady staring into mine. Neither of us looked away—hell, I don't know that we even blinked. Which, as twitchy as I was becoming due to the powerful lack of drugs in my system, was quite a feat. Finally, we both glanced away. Call it a stalemate.

"Fine. I'll square it. I want you gone, though. No point in having you around to complicate things. Fair?"

I nodded. I'll be honest, every piece of this felt slimy and gross, but I didn't see a better way around it. I had thought about just strolling away, letting Jamal burn this whole place down in his rage. But what if someone innocent had gotten hurt? I had thought, too, about just calling it in anonymously, but what if that got that nice bartender lady hurt? Or worse, me?

Telling Frank, I reckoned he would frame it up in a way that would protect him and his, which I hoped would also extend to both me and her. And if he was half the business man I thought he was, I knew he'd have no qualms about cutting Black Tom loose. The man had gone from a business opportunity to a liability with a quickness.

I hadn't even begun to try and parse my feelings on the whole matter of my daddy being such a horrible person. I mean, I intimately knew a litany of ways he was a grade A asshole, but this was on a different level. A *whole* different level. I was going to have to do a tremendous amount of drinking and drugging to fuck this out of my mind.

"Well, I guess you pay me, and I'll be on the road, then."

Frank pulled out an envelope from his desk and passed it to me. "Three thousand dollars."

I was pretty sure my eyes bulged. I hadn't expected *half* that much, but fuck was I glad for it, especially as my ride home was no longer an option. I reached out and grasped it hungrily, but he held the envelope tight.

"This much, it buys your silence, and I do mean not a fucking *peep* to anyone. And two more things: First, you let me handle this—no interfering. Two, I need you in the future, you come running. Understood?"

I acted like I was seriously considering what he had to say before finally nodding my agreement. In truth, he could've added any demands he'd wanted to that list; it wouldn't have mattered, not really. Because on the one hand I was not about to leave that office without that three grand, and on the other I had zero intention of holding up my end of any deal like that unless it directly benefited me. But Frank seemed happy enough, and he turned the money loose.

I didn't insult him by counting it in front of him. I had *some* tact, after all.

FAMILY TRADITION

Jackie-O was still sitting inside the car waiting on me when I came out. That money was burning a hole in my pocket, that's for damn sure. I don't think I've ever had so much money at one time in my whole life. I felt like I could buy all the goddamn drugs in the world.

But there was a little niggling thought digging around in my head. Just a tiny one, mind you, but one that kept interfering with my dreams of burying my face in a mountain of coke like Scarface. And that was the fact that I had car-buying money in my pocket.

It chapped my ass that the thought had even come to me—I blamed Anna for being a fucking good influence. A year ago, the thought would've never even crossed my fucking mind, and I could have happily blown every cent on one bus ticket and a shit ton of drugs. I did have a box of oblivion to replace, after all.

Slipping back into the passenger seat, I looked over at Jack. He was cranking the car, his usual smile written large across his face. "Bus station still the plan, cousin dearest?"

I frowned. "Fuck. Maybe."

Jack sat there, his hands on the wheel. "If not there, then where?"

My phone buzzed. It was a text from Anna, asking when I would be getting back. Pouting, I threw the phone to the floorboard. "Jack, you happen to know where I could buy a car for cheap?"

Jack laughed. "Frank paid better than you thought, eh? And I do, in fact. Hell, I'll sell you this one for cheap—on one condition."

"What's that?" I asked, about damn tired of folks and their *conditions.*

"I wanna go with you. I'm getting twitchy sitting 'round these parts waiting for the family to get rolling. I've a mind to meet some kin I've known, and see some sights I've never seen. Take me back with you to Jubal County, and in a couple months run me back this way if I haven't earned my way back into a car by then."

I looked the car over. It wasn't the best, but it would do, I supposed. "How much?"

"Two grand sound fair?"

That's when the haggling began. In the end it went for fifteen hundred bucks, plus my agreement to make a little detour on the way home.

Turned out that Mardi Gras was starting up, and New Orleans wasn't all that far off, really.

Mississippi Goes To Hell

DRIVING MARSH DAISY

Seeing as I owned the car now, you'd think I'd be the one driving. But in addition to buying said car, I had also scored some really killer drugs, and driving wasn't advisable for me at the moment. I wasn't tripping or anything too wild—yet—but the high I had cooking was not looking to come down anytime soon, so since the car had originally been Cousin Jack's anyway, I opted to be chauffeured around.

The car had come with a fairly impressive set of classic rock cassettes, so we were beginning our journey with Jimmy Page's wailing guitar blasting through the mostly busted speakers. They sounded like shit, to be honest, but with the sound of the wind coming through the open windows, it sorta muffled the worst of the crunchy rattling sounds. I'd heard worse over the years, and the fact that they now belonged to me made the sound just a little bit sweater.

I hadn't had a car in some time. When drugs are your number one priority, routine maintenance on a vehicle sometimes falls to the wayside. My last car, a ratty little S10, had slung a rod after I went about twenty thousand miles over the suggested mileage for an oil change. I had been far too high at the time to realize what had happened until the engine well and truly caught fire.

It might still be sitting on the side of the road, for all I know. In my drugged-up haze, I had just walked away from it, staggering through the night till I found my way home. How, exactly, I don't know. But the truck had died like it lived: hard and hot. Since it had given up the ghost in a fireball of glory, I'd never been able to muster up enough spare cash to buy a replacement because, well, drugs. Five hundred dollars for a barely running beater was better spent in ten dollar chunks on pills and powders, I'd long ago decided. And that mindset had kept me sinking for years now.

I blamed my girlfriend for my sudden spurt of responsibility. I swear she was doing something to me, threatening to bring out the best in me. Granted, my "best" tended to be fairly far below any normal person's worst, but even my oblivious ass was starting to notice. Even six months ago I would've just bought the cheapest bus ticket I could find and spent the difference on drugs. This new me, though? I'd bought a cheap car and spent the *leftover* on drugs. To be fair to the shitty me still lying dormant within, it was *a lot* of really good drugs—but even then I'd managed to save enough to put half a tank of gas in the car. It was so damn un-Marsh-like, I hardly knew what to think.

Of course, I had every intention of guiling Jack into using the money I had given him for the car to keep us well stocked on gas and smokes until I made it home to Jubal County . . . but I hadn't broken that fact to him yet. I intended to slowly guilt him into it over the next day or two, till I had him good and trained on where exactly he should set his expectations of my behavior.

For now, though, New Orleans and Mardi Gras awaited! I'd never been to either, but I knew my uncle Rooster lived out that way, so he would probably put us up for a couple days. If not, well, I wasn't above sleeping in a car. I'd already made sure to claim the back seat in case it came to that—owner's prerogative and all. The only thing raining on my proverbial parade was the sporadic bits of clucking coming from the back seat . . . even if it was mostly my fault.

I Think That Chicken Is Following Us

We'd just left Jack's hookup and were about to properly start our journey. Just had to get a little gas to get us rolling, was all, and then we'd be hitting the road. The gas station, though—the nearest one, that is—had us driving past where I'd just spent the last couple of days adventuring, as it were.

The Lagniappe Lounge passed us by on the left, and as we got closer to where we'd found the body I gave Jackie-O a little slap on the arm, asking him to slow down. I wanted to see how well I could see it from the road, and if you could see that pile of sand we'd left. Frank was giving me time to get outta town before he called in the crime, which was nice of him, even though I was sure it benefited him to have my loose end well out of sight and out of mind.

As we neared, something caught my eye, a bit of movement. And what I saw had me second-guessing on if the weed I'd just smoked had been laced with something a little stronger.

Racing along the treelike were three fairies riding on the backs of some roosters.

Each fairy looked different from the other, but there was no doubt they were all the same sort of creature: a bit under a foot tall, winged, and all sorts of shades of color. Each set of wings was totally different from the next, from feathered to leaf-like to something resembling a moth's. They were all sorta differently shaped, too, ranging from real fat to rail thin, but there was zero doubt: they were fairies.

The roosters had to be the fighting roosters we had freed. Why were fairies, who could fly faster than a chicken could run, riding them? Who the fuck knows. Maybe fairies are lazy. Maybe they just wanted to fuck with me.

Jack, I guess, hadn't seen them. I glanced at him to confirm that I was maybe not losing my mind, but his eyes were locked on the rearview mirror. "I think that chicken is following us," he said.

I looked back over my shoulder. Sure enough, running down the middle of the road after us, was a rooster. I wasn't certain, but it looked kinda like the one that had been so attached to me when I'd freed them. Which made about as much sense as fairies riding roosters, I reckoned, but then it was pretty clear things just couldn't be normal for even one fucking day of my life. "Stop the car," I groaned.

Jack obliged, not even bothering to ask questions. I think he had noticed the fairies, and that pretty well had his tongue all tied up. There weren't any cars coming—this was the middle of bumfuck nowhere, after all—so I stepped out onto the pavement. I didn't know exactly how fast a chicken could run, but this one had caught up to our stopped car by the time I'd managed to get good and out. Damn thing strutted right up to me, and I swear it just looked up at me, all expectant-like. And then after a couple of seconds of a stare down, with me not doing anything at all, the little shit pecked at my shoe. I jumped back a bit, startled. I mean, it hadn't pecked hard enough to get through my shoe, but I damn sure didn't want to be on the wrong side of a fighting cock if it decided it didn't like me all of a sudden. Them talons could hurt.

Now that I was out of the way, the rooster jumped in through the open door, up into my seat. Then, with a fluttery to-do of feathers, it launched itself into the back seat. Jack and I just looked at each other blankly. I don't think he knew what to say. I know I sure as hell didn't.

Those mounted fairies had vanished, it looked like. I couldn't see them anywhere anymore, at least. It didn't take a genius to make the connection—they had clearly helped set this up in some way. Whether it was some device of theirs or if that rooster really did like me and they owed it a favor, I don't reckon we'll ever know.

I just got back in the car, and we set back out with a new passenger. Some things, it's best to just roll with.

And the drugs sure helped with that.

On March the Saints

So, now riding three deep, we made our start. I was letting Jackie-O be the tour guide, as it were. These were his stomping grounds, and all I told him was that I wanted to see a bit of scenery. I didn't give much of a damn about where we went, especially as I had no intention to be paying for the gas. So, rather than making a bunch of stops where I might be lured into spending my money on shit that wasn't drugs, I wanted to see what Mississippi had to offer my eyes.

Because I was damn sure not looking to ever go back again. I was one and done with this state, no matter what promises I'd made to Frank.

I will admit, Mississippi felt real homey. I mean, from what I was seeing it was basically just like Jubal County, if perhaps a little less dingy, but there was still the rampant poverty that I felt so at home with everywhere you cared to look. We were taking backroads almost exclusively, which, given the amount of drugs we had in the car, was probably a smart move. But even beyond that, those are the places I wanted to see. The places I liked the most. I grew up in a county with more dirt roads than paved, and so the rural corners were what I could best relate to. And hell, if I wasn't getting rattled half to death by shitty roads meeting shitty shocks, was I even really in a vehicle?

We stopped about ten miles from Crainesboro at a closed-up gas station so Jackie could rock a piss around the side of it. It was a thing of broke-down beauty. Old cinderblocks, so old all the paint had flaked off years ago, with iron-braced windows with glass so thick that decades of kids' rocks had only managed to crack and hole a few of them. It squatted there beside the road like a gray toad, with two large holes in the roof for eyes.

I took a picture of it to send to Anna. One of the things I liked about her was she could see the beauty in things like this, too. Hell, that was probably why she stuck it out with me! Ain't a much more wretched thing in Jubal County than me. Getting a little bit of Jackie-O's bare ass in the corner of the shot was just the icing on the cake. Gotta throw in an Easter egg when you can—keep things interesting.

I kept staring at the gas station, even after my cousin had tucked himself away and gotten back into the car. It was a haunting sort of place, the kind where you could almost feel the veil slipping away. I had no doubt that if I came here on the right night or the correct time with some sort of offering, something fell and old would come out from the shadows of those broken windows. Or maybe come stalking up out of the forest that edged up toward the back of it.

There was a whole magical world out here beyond the bounds of Jubal County, and I had never really experienced it. I felt a sudden longing to see just what that might be like, to explore the little nooks and crannies where the things that went bump in the night dwelled. It wouldn't be the safest thing, but then neither was the amount of drugs I pumped into my body on a daily basis.

I wanted to see the places like this gas station when the magic came out to play. To see the rusted old pumps become a modern-day Stonehenge, all lit in the pale blue of flickering fairy light. To watch as creatures of shadow danced across the roof under the moonlight. It was my legacy to hold with such beings, and I was starting to feel like it was getting ever closer to time to really start living up to that.

I slipped back into the car. The chicken had still not shut up, but Jack had lit a joint, so that made things much more tolerable. He took a long drag, then passed it to me.

Soon, we were off again.

The Path We Choose Is Seldom Free of Leaves

In the end, I had to grab the wheel and snatch it to the right. Jack swore up a storm and had to rip the wheel back from me so we wouldn't go slamming into the trees. We did, however, go off the road a few feet, the passenger side tires off in the grass that lined the paved road.

"Are you fuckin' mad?!" he shouted as he got us to a stop. We were fully off the road now as he slammed it into park.

I shrugged. I probably was, but then he was the one who hadn't been listening to me. It was my car, and I didn't give a fuck if he was driving. If I wanted to stop, we were gonna stop. I had not a fuck to give about how bad an idea he might personally find it at that moment. "I said pull over."

He replied with something not very polite; I may have returned the sentiment. It got a little heated, and then it got a good bit more heated. Before I knew it we were standing in front of the car about six inches apart, shouting into each other's faces, when a third voice intruded. It was a good thing it did, or I'm pretty certain we'd have come to blows. And as I'm a scrawny little shit with not much in the way of fighting ability—which, considering my mouth, was not a good thing—that would likely have gone poorly for me.

"I hope this isn't on my account," said the voice.

That stopped both of us straight away. I turned, and sure enough it was the hitchhiker that had, in fact, started all this. When I had seen the man, I'd told Jackie-O to pull over so's we could give him a lift. My cousin had disagreed, him clearly not being filled with the same amount of Christian charity as myself, which led us to the current squabble—one that even I'd admit had gotten a bit out of hand. It was one hundred percent on that man's account, but this was the South; there was no way either of us would just outright admit that fact. "No, of course not," I said through gritted teeth, still side-eying my cousin. "Just a bit of a heated debate on lane usage."

The other man just nodded. This was my first time getting a look at him not while not going fifty-five miles an hour, and I had to admit, he was a little unsettling.

The first thing that stood out was how tall he was, and lanky. He was at least six-foot-four, maybe taller, but I doubted he weighed much above one sixty. He was pale as a sheet, just about, with hair so black that against his skin it might as well have been night made flesh. It was his eyes, though. They were dark—*real* dark. I'm not gonna say they were black, but they were so brown, they may as well have been. They had a way of staring right through you that was just . . . odd.

"Well, good. I'd hate to be the cause of any fuss," he said softly. His voice was like getting hit with a feather pillow. It was soft and cushiony, but it sorta struck you harder than you would've thought. Like a stage whisper, almost. "If you don't mind, I'll just slip on past you fine gentlemen, then."

He talked way too proper, I thought. It didn't match his look. He had on a clean pair of jeans over some snakeskin boots, and his shirt wouldn't have looked out of place on the stage of the Grand Ole Opry. It was deep red with all sorts of blue and black rhinestones dotting it, making these elaborate flower patterns. It all went along quite well with the guitar case he carried across his back. Looking like that, I would've thought the most country drawl you'd ever heard would have come out of his mouth, but no—it was like the man had no accent at all. *Well that's unsettling.*

I was now of a mind that maybe Jackie-O was right—that we should in no way give this man a lift. There was something off, and though I damn sure wasn't going to openly admit I was wrong, that didn't mean I had to now actually vocalize an offer of giving this man a lift. So, of course, because that's the sort of day it was turning out to be, Jack did. "Where ya headed? Might could give you a lift?"

A slow, broad grin that showed way too many teeth—good teeth, mind you, but not *distractingly* good teeth—split the man's face. "I'm heading to Drew, if you are going that way."

I had no idea where Drew was, but if this man was going there, I was pretty sure I didn't want to be. "Well . . ." I started to say, planning to nip this in the bud.

"Sure thing," Jackie said, cutting me off. "We're not heading anywhere in particular. May as well go by way of Drew as any other. It'll let Marsh here see a bit of the Delta."

And that's how we wound up riding four deep to Drew. The tall man didn't seem to mind the chicken; he just kept his guitar case between them, and finally that damn rooster actually shut the fuck up.

So there was that, at least.

Ramblin' On My Mind

It was right awkward in the car for a few moments as we got back up to speed. No one said anything, and the longer no one said anything, the more awkward it got. Usually I would've tried to chat the man up, see what was taking him to wherever it was we were headed or where he'd come from. But where I had been mildly creeped out before when he was outside the car, now that he was seated behind me I was doubly so. I kept imagining those long, pale fingers wrapping around my throat.

"Would you be opposed to some music?" the tall man asked from the back.

I heard the clasps on the guitar case snap, and I turned my head to see what was going on. Instead of a guitar, though, inside were dozens of tape cassettes. None had covers, but down the side each had a piece of yellowing tape with a name written in red ink. There looked to be dozens, maybe hundreds of 'em.

"Pick your poison!" the man exclaimed, waving a hand across his collection. I'll be honest, most of them I didn't know, but there were a few I did recognize. Bob Dylan was in there, and so was Jimmy Page. I thought it was weird that it had just Jimmy Page and not Led Zeppelin, but then everything about this was weird. Who the fuck carried around cassettes these days? I mean, sure, my car had a tape deck, but what were the odds of that, really?

"I think we're good, man," I ended up saying, pulling my eyes from the case to look back to the road. I reached up and clicked the tape deck on, and AC/DC started piping through the ratty speakers. It was some deep-cut album I didn't know, but it was better than touching anything that weirdo might've had.

Clearly ol' boy knew it, however, as he took to sorta humming along real low. Worse, he took those long fingers of his and was tapping them on his guitar case in time with the tunes. I turned up the music a bit to try and drown it out, but damned if it didn't seem to just bore right into my head. *Tap. Tap. Tap. Tappity tappity tap. Tap. Tap. Tap. Tappity tappity tap. Tap. Tap.*

I cut off the music hard enough that for a moment I thought I might've snapped off the knob. Behind me, our guest broke into a chuckle. It sounded like leaves rustling over asphalt, and I'll be damned if I didn't want to turn around and just smack the taste outta that man's mouth. I held it together, though, somehow. I really can be a saint sometimes.

I heard the damn guitar case clasps pop open again. I'm not gonna lie, I sorta went to eleven when I heard them—that man offering up another one of his damn bootleg tapes was likely going to end with me in jail. As comfortable as I'd become with frequent stops in the Jubal County jailhouse, I had no desire to see what a Mississippi prison was like.

I whipped my head around to tell our erstwhile visitor just what he could do with those tapes, but what I saw stopped me dead in my tracks. That bastard was pulling a slick blue-and-black guitar out of that same case. A case I'd seen inside of just a few moments earlier, and that there had, in fact, *not* been a guitar in. What I was seeing was impossible.

But then again, the impossible made real was the weird limbo I tended to find my life occupying more often than not, and whenever I came across it, that almost always meant I was about to be in some shit. As I sat there staring, my jaw dropped open, and I knew that nothing good was gonna come of this.

"They told me you were a contrary little shit, Howard Marsh," the man said as he began tuning his guitar.

Plucking the strings, he slowly spun the pegs, tightening or loosening each in turn. He had his head cocked as he did it, listening closely till each sounded just right.

I looked over at Jackie-O. I didn't think he had realized anything was wrong till this stranger had said my full name. I could see the dawning realization that we'd let the fox in the henhouse creep over his face, and his fingers tightened on the wheel.

"Who's 'they'?" I managed to get out, trying to loosen up the grip fear had on my heart just then. My voice sounded small, I thought, but I didn't really hold it against myself just then. The man looked dead at me, those eyes just digging into my soul and rootin' around. I swear I could feel him turning up all the rocks I'd hidden my deepest, darkest secrets under, pawing over them like a greedy banker over gold coins.

"A colleague of mine," he grinned. For the first time, I noticed silver caps on his canines, one which glinted with a tiny red dot.

A ruby? Who fucking knew. I didn't stare, even though I wanted to. I was too busy focusing on the smell of cooking bacon filling my nostrils.

"The Hog of the Road," I said. It wasn't a question; I knew as soon as I'd smelled that succulent pork. The Hog was a demon, and if this "man" was a colleague of theirs, then we'd just let a fucking demon into the car.

The demon's smile deepened. "Just so. When I heard you were in my area, well, I just had to come take a look. And since you were kind enough to offer me an invitation to accompany you . . ."

"Marsh—" Jackie started. I could feel him take his foot off the gas, no doubt thinking to start hitting the brakes.

Our guest cut him off. "Just keep driving, if you know what's good for you."

Jackie looked at me, and I gave a small nod. He eased his foot back on the gas, but his hands didn't loosen, judging from how white his knuckles were. I just turned my focus back on our guest. He had finished tuning and was beginning to pick out some sort of bluesy riff. I didn't recognize it, but then I'm not a blues man. It didn't sound like a happy tune, though, that much was clear. The man just kept his head down, bobbing it slightly in time with the song, his long hair falling over his face.

Then he started to sing. His voice was a little thinner than I would've thought, with a sort of breathy huskiness that underlay it. Each line, he ended with a little quiver of vibrato that was haunting in its emotion. The words, though, were what chilled me to my soul.

"I got to keep moving, I got to keep moving.

Blues falling down like hail, blues falling down like hail.

Mmm, blues falling down like hail, blues falling down like hail."

He looked up then, still singing, his hair framing his too thin, too pale face. Silver flashed as he smirked.

"And the day keeps on remindin' me, there's a hellhound on my trail.

Hellhound on my trail, hellhound on my trail."

The Crossroad Blues

He stopped singing but his fingers kept up the music, sliding across the strings with a sinuous grace. "I'll admit, I haven't heard a lot about you, Howard Marsh. But the things I have . . . you've made some waves, haven't you?"

"I don't guess I can say the same about you. Just who the hell are you?" I was trying to come off as being in control, but I didn't really think I was pulling it off. My experience with demons was extremely limited, mostly just to the Hog of the Road.

The demon flashed a grin. "That song I was just playing, it was by a man named Robert Johnson. Ever hear of him?"

I slowly shook my head.

"I have," Jackie said. "Blues guy. Sold his soul to the devil to play guitar, they say. Sort of a Mississippi legend."

"Just so. Though most folks don't realize that the legend is also attributed to Tommy Johnson, another blues legend, but of no relation to Mr. Robert. Tommy, they say, met the devil at a crossroads; Robert, in a graveyard that he liked to practice in. I am here to tell you that in this case, what 'they' say is, in fact, correct." The demon raised a hand and tipped an imaginary cap. The guitar kept playing as he did it. "You can call me Cross. Though Robert, when he wrote a song about me, he decided I'd best be known as Hellhound. So, pick your poison." he winked.

"Wordy sumbitch, ain't ya?"

Cross roared with laughter at that. "Oh, Howard Marsh, you are even better than they said! This is going to be an absolute delight, I think."

I didn't like the sound of that. At all. "This? What's 'this'?"

The music stopped then, and Cross placed both hands on the neck of the guitar. He locked eyes with me, and the smile faded. For the first time I could clearly see the devil in him. Deep in his eyes were tiny sparks of flame, sparks that seemed to grow larger the longer I looked. His face darkened and became more lined. Shadows deepened under his eyes, and his teeth became sharper, more lethal looking. His pale flesh took on a sickly pallor, like a corpse, with blue veins under the skin showing up brilliantly under paper-thin skin. His nails darkened and grew till they were like small blood-colored claws. And his hair, which had been dark already, somehow grew even more so. It looked heavy, dense, like it was sucking up the light.

"Well, you two are taking me to Drew, of course. And if you show me a good enough time, then at the end of the ride I will even be so kind as to let one, or maybe even both, of you leave with your soul, since neither of you are true musicians. But you had best make a damn fine showing if you want that to happen."

We were well and truly fucked. There was no way a demon would let someone get out of their grasp—not someone like me, at least. I wasn't even sure how a creature like him could be running around loose at all. Usually they had to be called up and set to a specific purpose, and under very strict rules, or bad shit usually happened to whoever did the calling up.

I didn't have enough magic in me, nor the know-how, to take down a thing like Cross. Not one on one, in a straight-up fight—just plumb couldn't do it. Most of my magic, he'd probably just shrug off; the rest he'd blast back in my face. At least that's what my uncle had always said.

"I like music, and I like stories. Keep your entertainment in that wheelhouse, and you stand a chance. Not a large one, of course, but at least it's something." He took a deep breath through his nose, then sighed. "Ahh, the scent of hope. Delicious."

"There any sort of rules?" I asked. Demons loved rules.

Cross shook his head in what was clearly mock sadness, which his tone backed up. "There would be rules if this was a contest, of course. All 'Devil Went Down to Georgia' style and everything. But contests have to be declared from the start, and frankly, you don't have any leverage." He leaned back, lacing his fingers behind his head. "Now, entertain me, peasants, and beg that you may live."

Wear a Suit of Red and White

"I don't guess you'd just let me dip out real quick, would ya? I barely know this jack-off, and it seems like he's who you really want," Jackie asked from the driver's side. "I know how to keep my mouth shut."

"Fucking really?" I swore at him. I didn't blame him in the least, though. I was even then trying to judge if I could survive a tuck and roll out the car door. We were going a bit too fast for all that, but if we slowed enough, I thought I might give it a go. I liked having a car, but I also was really fond of having my soul firmly in my body. We'd grown attached, you might say.

Cross laughed. "Sorry, you need to learn to choose better friends. And before anyone gets any bright ideas . . ."

All the locks, which were manual, mind you, clicked down. The bastard had locked us in. *So much for abandoning ship.* I wanted to be angry, real angry, but I was too scared, to be perfectly honest. I'd been in tight spots before, and a bunch that were more immediately dangerous. But there was something different about knowing you were going to die in a few hours and there was nothing you could do to stop it . . .

I felt like throwing up.

Jackie was clearly in a similar sort of mood. He took to being a bit dramatic, as they'd say biblically, sorta wailing and gnashing his teeth. Really just causing a scene. A fair bit of it was even directed toward me, as though I was the one that had invited the fucking demon in in the first place. Just really classless, if you ask me.

Once he got done venting his spleen and was able to talk like a regular person again, having cursed me and Cross every which way but up, he managed to offer up an actual suggestion. To be fair, I had been a bit too deep in "wallow in pity" mode to really think about how we might try and entertain a demon.

Which was dumb of me. Even if I was sure that Cross was gonna snatch our souls no matter what we did, having an unhappy demon in the back seat wasn't good for anyone's health. I could see the boredom beginning to creep onto the demon's face as he listened to us squabble. Some demons would have just lapped that up, but Cross was clearly cut from a different kind of cloth.

"Can I stop the car long enough for Marsh and me to switch seats? If you'll loan me that guitar, I can pluck a few tunes for you," offered Jackie-O.

"Be my guest. Anything if it will stop the incessant whining."

Jack slowed the car down and pulled over onto the grass. I hadn't exactly agreed to this, but since I wasn't exactly offering up suggestions, I just went with it. It was awkward, us moving around each other to get situated, but with only a few heated words exchanged we got settled. I wasn't high anymore, which was a very mixed blessing in that moment, so as I put the car in drive I started thinking about how I might contribute.

Cross handed up his guitar, and Jackie let loose a low whistle. "This is a mighty fine guitar you got here, Mr. Cross."

I couldn't see the demon directly anymore, my eyes being mostly on the road. But there was a dingy rearview mirror, so I took to glancing in it every so often, and every fucking time Cross would be staring right back at me. It was mighty unsettling.

Jackie-O reached around and pulled out his wallet and, digging through it, produced a pick. I'd had no idea the man could play, but then what did I really know about the guy? I'd only known him a couple days, and though he seemed like a good sort, this sorta made me come to the realization that I had climbed in bed with what was effectively a stranger just because he was kin. Hell, I didn't even have any real proof of that, even.

That was a problem for later, though.

Wallet tucked back in his pants, Jack began to play. He didn't sing as he strummed the strings, but he did hum along. Whatever it was, it was soulful, bluesy, and damn good. I'd have never guessed he was as good as he was showing himself to be.

Cross leaned forward, and for the first time he closed his eyes. He sat there, propped across his guitar case, slowly bobbing his head in time with the music. Every so often he'd hum along, or sing a word or two under his breath. Rather than getting on my nerves, it was actually a good accompaniment to the music. It was like the two were doing a wordless duet, singing a secret song or something.

The music flowing from those fingers was melancholy, carrying a sadness that words would have only cheapened, I thought. It made me think of someone shedding lonesome tears but trying not to let anyone know. If a guitar could weep, that one would have been.

I wondered if Jackie-O might have a touch of the gift, but reaching out with my magic a bit, I didn't feel anything.

That opened up Cross's eyes. "Easy now, Howard Marsh, easy. It's just music," he said softly.

I shut that shit down quick. I hadn't banked on just how sensitive Cross would be to magic; he'd picked up on even that tiny little tendril right away. That fairly well dashed the tiny little bud of hope I had allowed to spark that maybe I could do something. Not bothering to address Cross, I looked over at Jack. "You're gonna need to tell me where the fuck we're going if I'm gonna be doing the driving."

We rode like that for about an hour, me driving, Jack playing. The only words spoken were the occasional direction from my copilot telling me which turn to take. He never did start singing, and after about forty-five minutes Cross stopped humming along. Glancing in the mirror, it was clear our boy was getting bored. He wasn't paying Jackie any attention, really. He'd even stopped freaking me out by matching my glances in the window. Instead, he just sort of stared out the window or over at the chicken.

The chicken was the only one acting normal—normal enough for a random rooster in someone's back seat, I guess. It just sat there steadily clucking along. It did peck the hand of Cross the one time he tried to touch the thing, which, rather than making him angry like I would've thought, just elicited a laugh.

No one wants a bored demon on their hands, even when souls aren't on the line. Idle hands and all that, right? So I knew it was time for me to step up. I'd spent the last little while pondering what story to tell and how to go about it—something that would keep Cross happy—and I knew I had just the story.

"Alright, Jack, how 'bout you give it a rest for a bit? It's story time with Unkie Marsh now."

Jack pulled his hands from the strings, and I noticed how they curled. He'd about played them out and looked to be in a fair bit of pain. I felt a little guilty for not noticing before then, but I was reminded how he'd gotten us into this in the first place and decided that karma was outside my purview. He could stretch them out by taking over driving, I decided. "Swap seats with me real quick."

Once we were all rearranged and settled in, the devil spoke. "Alright, let's hear what you've got," Cross said, turning his head from the window to face me.

"You like music, and you like stories. Well, this story is all about music. Let me tell you about the first time I met my friend Johnny . . ."

Story Time with Howard Marsh: Johnny and the Neck

I cracked open my fifth beer of the day as I watched the dust settle. Billy Mack, my soon-to-be-former landlord, had just left after handing me an eviction notice. I was pissed, of course, but I was even more pissed that he had come knocking on my door at seven in the morning. Any normal person would have been asleep, and he should have known that. Just rude.

Of course, I hadn't slept in a while. I had settled into getting a good drunk spell going so that I could get some sleep, but now that he had gone and riled me up, that didn't seem too likely. A half hour of yelling wasn't real conducive to getting me in a restful state.

Literally pissing on his eviction notice right in front of the man might have been a step too far, though. That, I will admit. It was too damn early in the day to go whippin' your dick out in front of somebody, even if they were kicking you out of your home over something as petty as late rent.

Really, I'd been doing the man a favor, keeping the place occupied. The trailer I called home was so ratty and tore up, I wouldn't have let a dog live in there with me—holes in the floor, plumbing that worked only when it felt so inclined, no air conditioning since someone had stole the copper out of it for drug money . . . place was a mess. The sporadic money I gave him was better than nothing. He'd play hell finding anyone other than a meth cook willing to take on the place, so it was really just him biting off his nose to spite his face. Just dumb as hell.

I mean, I'd paid half rent at least two out of the five months I'd been living there. And I bet you the bastard was already planning to keep my deposit as some sort of bullshit "cleaning fee" or something. Those roaches were mostly already there when I moved in, anyway.

All in all it was a piss-poor morning to cap off a piss-poor week. I'd not gotten half as much money for that copper as I thought I would've, and the engine in my car had blown slam up. I couldn't even tell you where the damn thing was, which pissed me off even more. There was some good scrap money to be had off that car, I bet, but damned if I could remember how I got home, much less where I had got home from.

If I'd had a phone I would've called up Lidda, tried to dip my wick. But I didn't, and I also didn't really have enough goodies to share with her, which she would want to do. Maybe I would get lucky and she would swing by to check in. It was as good a reason to stay up drinking as any, I reckoned. The ice in my cooler had all melted anyway, and I knew I'd need to drink up what was left of this twelver before it got too hot and they went skunky.

Day successfully planned, I leaned back in the plastic lawn chair I had sat in the shade of an old oak tree and settled in to do some serious drinking. I had a half bottle of gin tucked away somewhere in the trailer, I thought; maybe I would get up the gumption to battle the roaches and try and find it. That was a project for later, though. I was sure I would want a good drunk already in full bloom before I braved the mess.

The trailer was a rusted mess, and the yard was either covered in trash and junk or was just a dirt patch, but it was still a pretty day. It was a rare spring morning that actually felt like spring. At seven thirty in the morning I wasn't dripping sweat, and any day I can say that, I count as a victory. The beer, while not cold, was at least not fully warm yet, so this was about as close to paradise as I'd found myself in some time.

A fat joint would've really just made it all just pop, but I was slap out of weed. I'd set aside my last forty bucks for drugs, and if I could find a way to get to where they were,

I would be in good shape for a couple days. Not having a car was really starting to harsh what little of my mellow I was trying to retain.

As if the universe had heard my thoughts I heard the muted sounds of an engine coming down the dirt road. I wasn't the last house on the road, but I was damn near it, so it was about even odds that whoever it was, was coming to see me. That was a short list of people—mainly Lidda and Hubert Dale—but either of them would do in a pinch, seeing as they had cars and an ability to be annoyed into submission by me.

I prayed right then. Not to anyone or anything, really—I ain't no hypocrite. Well, at least not in that regard. It was just sorta me throwing my wish out there into the world that whoever was coming could take me away from this place. And take me to get drugs.

I got to my feet to show just how serious I was taking it all when I realized I'd maybe had a few more to drink than I remembered; I was just a nudge unsteady on my feet. Glancing over, I saw there had to be at least eight freshly crushed cans in a pile by my chair. I thought, "When the hell had that happened?"

That car was coming on closer and closer, and I'm not ashamed to admit I let out a little whoop of joy when I heard it turn up my driveway. It was a long drive, long enough they wouldn't hear me, but fuck, I was excited. I was about to be in business. I slapped my ass to make sure my wallet was there, and feeling its small bulge against my cheek made me one happy camper. If I'd been held up having to find my wallet, I might would've cried.

There were two beers left after I pounded back the one in my hand. That would be just right: one road beer there, one road beer back, then I could hit the drugs and gin. End my day on a high note.

The car that finally hove into view, though, was not HD's van, nor Lidda's run-down Geo. It was a dark-red Ranger about half covered in black mud that I didn't recognize. The way the sun was hitting the windshield, I couldn't tell exactly who was driving other than that they were male, whoever they were. I was suddenly a lot less pleased. Normally I would have walked across the yard and been a mite bit more welcoming, but I wasn't overly fond of strangers. Strangers could mean a lot of things—some good, but more often than not they meant work. I had a reputation as a finder of lost things and a water witch, which had people coming knocking on occasion. But that meant work, and I wasn't feeling work at that particular junction.

The man who got out of that truck was tall, and sorta disgustingly good-looking. Like, some sort of model good-looking. As he started coming across the yard, he smiled warmly, and that's when it clicked. I did know this guy, but only loosely. He'd been a few grades ahead of me back when I'd been in school, but his name escaped me. He was maybe some sort of musician? I had a faint memory of that.

"Howard Marsh?" he called out.

He'd kept the door open with one hand on it, I supposed in case I ended up not being who he thought I was. I toyed for a moment with telling him that I was not, in fact, Howard Marsh, but by this point I'd be lying if my curiosity hadn't gotten the better of me. "Yeah."

He shut the truck door and took to walking in my direction with a long, smooth stride. As he neared, he extended a hand. I looked at it a second before relenting and, after a quick wipe of my hand on my pants, shook his. The shake was firm, but not too firm. That was a good sign, I thought.

"You might not remember me, but I think we went to school together for a little while. I'm Johnny Erikson."

The name slipped right into place in my memory. "Yep, I remember you. So, what brings you out my way?"

To be southerly, I should've drawn out the small talk. Sorta eased us into chatting together, makin' everyone all comfortable and shit. And if I had been in a better mood, I might would have obliged. But I'd had a shit morning, and Johnny had had the poor luck to be the person I next ran into that couldn't immediately benefit me. So I said fuck comfort.

For the first time, Johnny's cool facade cracked a little. There were some nerves at work underneath all those model looks, and I had skipped the script. He was a little off-footed now, and he wasn't sure how to handle it. He opened his mouth twice, closing it both times before he finally spoke. "Damn, now that I'm actually here it all seems just really, really stupid." He looked down at his feet, then back up at me. "I think I'll just go before I make more of a fool of myself. Sorry to bother you."

He extended his hand out again, but when I made no move to shake it back this time, he just sort of awkwardly took it back and turned to leave. I let him get halfway to the truck before my damn mouth got me back involved. "Hold up," I sighed.

He paused, turning back around.

"Tell me what weird shit you think I can help with. I ain't got all day."

Looking at me real hard, he sorta gave his head a little shake. "You're probably gonna think it's stupid."

I definitely would—there was no doubt of that. But my Southern training had kicked in. "Oh, I doubt that."

He walked back over, but didn't get as close this time. He stopped right inside the shade, just so that all of him was out of the sun. He didn't bother extending a hand this time, for which I was grateful. "Well . . . I had this whole spiel figured out in my head on my way over. Sorta worked it out how to say it, but now that I'm here . . ." he grinned, and damn if he just wasn't fucking pretty. The kind of good-looking face you just hated to disappoint.

"Why not just give it to me like you practiced?"

He nodded, still grinning that shy sorta grin. "Fair. So, you may remember that I play the fiddle. My momma, she's had me taking violin lessons about since I could walk, always wanted me to be some sort of concert player, I think, like her grandmomma was. Well, I took to it pretty fine, though it'd be more accurate to say I play the fiddle. That concert style of music, it just don't appeal, but I love me some bluegrass and stuff like Mumford and Sons, the Avett Brothers, Trampled by Turtles, hell, all those kinda bands."

I knew the type, and my memory did confirm that he was a pretty good player. Memory said that was why I remembered him, in fact, that I had seen him play in a pasture party. He'd been good, even if it wasn't quite what I listened to at the time.

"I want to get better, though, and not to be that guy, but I have pretty well learned what my teachers can teach me. I have played a few of these bluegrass jams, and when it comes to fiddlin', there isn't really anyone better than me around here, at least not that I've been able to find. But I know there's more, I can feel it. It's . . . I can't explain it. But I know I got more to offer, if I can just unlock it."

I held up both hands, palms out. "If you think I got some spell that is gonna make you Charlie Daniels reborn or something, you're gonna be sorely disappointed."

His eyes sorta widened at that. "A spell? I didn't . . . I think I may have been kindly misinformed about you. Maybe. I just wanted to know if you'd ever heard of a nacken? And, if so, if they was real?"

The way he said it, I think it was probably spelled some sort of funny way, but it sounded like *nah-ken*, like someone knockin' on a door. In which case, I hadn't. Unless .. . "You mean a knocker?"

At that Johnny, shook his head. "Oh, no, I've heard of them too. My great-granddad, he was from Sweden, like off the boat. He would always tell all these funny stories about knockers pulling pranks down in the mines back in the old country. But he also told me once about a nacken, not too long before he died. He actually called me one as a joke, I think, then told me a little about them. Some sort of critter that lived in the river, but it was hell on a fiddle, and if you asked it nice it could show you a few tricks."

This was a new one on me. If I'd ever been told about one, it would've been before my lessons stopped, and there was a whole lot of grief and drugs between me and those years.

My mind was coming up blank. But that wasn't what was worrying me.

"Why do you think such a thing would be real in the first place? Fairy tales are just that," I said. I'd never met anyone who wasn't fully fucking crazy, or who had some magic, that actually believed in anything like this. Johnny seemed like the kind of guy who just sorta coasted through life on good looks and a ready smile, but this whole thing had him out of sorts. I could tell he was real hesitant to talk about this, and if I had been anyone of note in his life, I got the feeling I would never have heard about it. He was back staring at his feet again, acting like I'd caught him with his hand in the cookie jar.

"You promise you ain't gonna laugh at me?"

I slowly nodded, but when I realized he wasn't looking at me, I said, "Promise."

"I went looking for one. You see, sometimes when I play, I think . . . I think I do a little magic. Like, well, I don't know—it's just something special sometimes. And if I can do that, I got to thinking maybe some of those stories about the knockers and the nacken, they might be real. My great-granddad, he wasn't a liar, and he always acted like these stories was real and all. So, I went lookin."

"Well, I don't wanna burst your bubble—" I started, but he cut me off.

"I think I found one. And I want to hire you to help me figure out how to get it to teach me how to play."

Interlude: "Cause They Smile, and Tell Him Lies"

I had sorta forgotten what a huge piece of shit I'd been back then. I was still a shitty guy, but I wasn't *that* bad nowadays, I thought. Thinking back to how I had treated Johnny that day—a guy who would turn out to be one of the few folks I actually gave a shit about . . . well, it made me cringe inwardly.

I'd abruptly paused in my storytelling under the guise of rolling a joint. I needed to judge my audience, at least the half of it that mattered just then. I needed to know if I had Cross even a little entertained, otherwise we might as well have just stopped the car and let him have at us.

Jackie-O sorta nervously glanced my way as I was grinding the weed, getting it ready to roll. I was acting like I hadn't even noticed I'd stopped partway through my tale, like I had just absentmindedly focused on the joint. One glance became two, then three, and I saw him open his mouth to say something, but the first words I heard came from the back seat.

"Well?" Cross said.

I judged there was a hint of annoyance in his tone. This was good. That meant he cared enough about what I was saying to pay attention, and that he wanted to hear more. I was loath to dive back into that period of time in my life, but when life gives you demons . . .

Story Time with Howard Marsh: Catching a Ride

Years Ago

I think my jaw dropped just then, but I covered it by killing the beer in my hand. I bought myself a little thinking time by crushing the can and artfully, drunkenly, missing the crushed can pile by a good three feet.

"Well, fuck me, then. And how exactly . . ." I sorta waved my arm around in a looping swirl.

"Well, the story went that it likes rivers and streams. That it lives in them. So, I got to thinking about how legends and stuff, they always have something that was a seed of truth about them, no matter how weird a story they turned into. And if—"

"Stop. Just stop for a second." I went and sat back down in my chair. "So you think magic is real, because you can do 'something' when you play music. And because of that, this *thing* that your great-grandad told you about once from the old country must be real. You'll have to forgive me if I call bullshit. Normal people ain't like that. Not in my experience."

Johnny's face sorta hardened for a second. "I'm not lying."

I shook my head and sighed. "Not saying you are. But before we go any farther, I need to know something." I closed my eyes and started calling up my magic. I was pretty dry of drugs in my system—the little bit that was lingering wasn't much help—so I was calling on the tiny bit of natural power I had on hand.

"What's that?" he asked after I had been quiet a couple of seconds.

"Shhh," I hissed at him before he could wreck my concentration any further. Drunk as I was, this wasn't the easiest thing. A bump of coke, a crack rock, bit of meth, some pills, some shrooms, a fat joint—all that gave me at least something to call on, but being drunk just made things harder. Finally, I was able to get the power wrangled and, with a bit of effort, managed to get it directed at Johnny. It flowed out, invisible to the naked eye, but soon was pawing all over the man, metaphorically speaking. Sure enough, I found what I'd suspected I would: a tiny seed of power.

It was the same sort of seed my uncle HD had that made it so he always managed to know when he was going to be needed. A spark that gave a little specific power, but not enough to let a body actually learn magic like I had. It reminded me most of my uncle Rooster, though. He had a seed of power like that, and his was related to music as well. Things had initially gone a bit poorly for him, they said, before he was able to get a proper handle on things. But that was all before my time.

Regardless, a little seed like that, it opened you up to the magical world that had settled in the cracks and shadows of the world all around us. With anyone else, I would've guessed that they were full of shit, most likely, or just really confused. But Johnny . . . well, it was possible he actually had "found" whatever it was he was looking for. Though I suspected that instead of him finding it, it had found him, sensing his longing.

But what did I know? I was just a meth-head wizard.

I opened my eyes. "Ok, I'm more ready to listen. Tell me how you found this nacken thing."

He gave me an odd look but carried on. "Well, like I was saying, I had this thought. Legends all have seeds of truth, and I knew where there was a crybaby bridge, like they always talk about in urban legends and such. I don't believe in crybaby bridges, but I figured that something weird had likely happened there at some point. Maybe the 'veil' was thin there or something."

The only veil that existed was inside most people's minds, I'd learned long ago. But I didn't correct him.

"So I went there and just sat there on the tailgate of my truck and took to playing. I played and played for, like, hours. Till my fingers were about numb. About the time I gave up, though, I heard it."

He paused there for what was clearly supposed to be dramatic effect, but I just used the lull to open my last beer. When I didn't rise to the occasion, he just carried on.

"Off in the distance, down the creek, I heard something playing a fiddle back at me. Anything I would play, it would play, but better. One time I fucking cried, it was so beautiful. And that's how I knew it had to be something supernatural. If not a nacken, it had to be something like that. But even though I tried and tried, I couldn't get it to come any closer."

All in all, it sounded like something I could maybe work with. I wasn't sure I wanted to, though. I had never met a nacken, or anything that spent its time playing fiddles near creeks, but things like that rarely interacted on the up-and-up. They always wanted something, and that something was never good for whoever they was dealing with. I needed to know more first—that much was clear.

"So, how much money we talking here?"

Johnny pulled out his wallet from his back pocket and held it up. "I got a hundred bucks here if you can get me in contact with that thing, and another two hundred if it teaches me anything worth a damn."

Welp, that was all I needed to know. "Agreed, only let's call it a hundred bucks plus some expenses."

He frowned. "I don't make a lot of money . . . how much in expenses are you talking about?"

I grinned. "A pack of smokes, a twelve pack of something cheap, and you need to take me two places. Neither is far out the way."

Johnny thought for a second, then nodded his head. "Deal."

Finally, I had my ride.

Story Time with Howard Marsh: Got a Neck in My Creek

Years Ago

On some level, I suppose I should have realized that all this would lead to me trekking through some marshy bullshit. I was told clear as day that he thought this thing lived near a bridge. I should have put two and two together and come to the conclusion that this would entail trekking down the side of a stream—a thing I very much did not want to do.

So to say I was in a bit of a foul mood would be a massive understatement. The whole day had just been a roller-coaster of bullshit: Got served with an eviction—found a way to make some money. Slap out of good drugs, beer and smokes—found a ride to the gas station. Finally got some drugs—freaked out my client when I fired up my glass pipe in his car. Get preached at by Uncle Hubert Dale for never taking the time to learn about all this magic bullshit—learn something useful. Up and down, up and down, all fucking day.

And now it was back down, with me slapping at a swarm of mosquitos that had decided I was the tastiest thing since God invented Zebra Cakes.

Fuck, I wanted a Zebra Cake.

Johnny was leading the way. We'd parked the truck just before the bridge, on the side of the road. HD had told me that for whatever weird reason, your best bet to contact these things was on a Thursday, and today luckily being that, we were making for the direction Johnny had first heard the fiddle playing.

He had his case with him, but he hadn't gotten his instrument out yet. He was afraid of dropping it in the water, so we'd agreed after we trekked about half a mile that only then would he get it out and give it a strum.

HD hadn't known much beyond the whole Thursday thing, but he claimed he knew where to get more information about it. I wasn't of a mind to wait, wanting mostly to just get home and do more of my drugs in peace, so we'd left before he could find anything more. I figured if the thing was dangerous, he'd have remembered it. He had a good memory for shit like that usually, which is why I didn't feel much motivated to waste my time waiting on him to track down every little snippet he could.

'Cause let's be honest, he'd probably go dig through a bunch of Granny's books, and that always set me off because she'd never let *me* have a look at them. She had me where she wanted me: useful enough to handle her light weight, but not knowing enough to risk messing up her plans . . . whatever they were. I was extra pissed thinking about it because while actually putting in the effort to learn bona fide magic was more or less beyond me these days, I did have a bit of a passion for learning about magical critters. I just didn't have fuck all for resources to learn about them.

When I was younger, I'd sorta raged about that, being denied what by rights could have been mine. The drugs had helped dull that right down. Now, I had more pressing matters than learning the ins and outs of how my powers worked. Do drugs, sling spells—done.

I almost walked into Johnny's backside, so lost in my pity party I was. I managed to catch myself, though, and ended up kindly curving around him like I'd meant to do that the whole time. He was hunched over, opening up his case, so I guess we'd come far enough as he judged things. Leaning up against a tree, I settled in to watch. It wasn't a bad scene, all things considered. The stream was making a sorta pleasing flowing noise about twenty feet away. The trees were providing a good bit of shade, and even the walk hadn't really gotten me all that sweaty, that blessed spring air doing me a favor there.

Johnny had taken out the fiddle, and after a quick tune, he began playing. He started slow at first, not sad-like, just steady. The longer he played, though, the more jaunty things started to get. This was old-style bluegrass, like you might hear at a church social at one of the older churches in the county. And he played it damn good.

I worked up a little magic, using a nudge of drug juice to speed things along, and felt around the man. That little spark I'd found in him earlier was growing a bit, like someone breathing on coals to get a fire back started up. It wasn't like he was becoming a big power or anything, but it was noticeable. He was right—when it came to music, he did have power. And not an unappreciable amount, if I was any sort of judge. It wasn't my kinda music, but the way he played it, well, I didn't mind so much.

But if just him playing would've made this whole thing work, he'd have never needed to bring me along; he'd have like as not wandered right up to this "neck" thingy. But that hadn't been the case the last time he'd gone hunting it, so it was time for me to earn my keep, I reckoned.

My guess was that though he had a little power, enough that he could get hints of the hidden things of the world, it wasn't enough to fully punch through. Enough to get him into a little trouble now and then, but nothing like the way I was as much able to see into those dark magical corners without even trying, for good or ill. He needed me along to cut through the veil, which I thought might work just from me being along for the ride. There was every chance in the world that Johnny had walked right by this thing without ever seeing it, and only his connection to music-based power had allowed him to hear the thing.

But I wasn't gonna hedge my bets. I wasn't gonna put myself out a lot, but I thought I could try and burn a little of my own magic, see if I couldn't amp up his power a nudge. So, I fed a bit more magic into the working that I had done to see just what sort of energy his playing might have. This turned it from a questioning, searching type of connection to something that was feeding, pushing, filling. The music sounded no different to me, but I thought it would be a bit more punchy to any ears that were more in tune with the occult than my own.

Or maybe it wasn't doing jack shit. But I had at least done something—other than get mud on my shoes, that is—so I reckoned I was earning my keep. Or maybe I wasn't . . . I didn't much care, to be honest.

I wasn't sure how long we might have to sit there, and I was real torn on starting to roll a joint or not. I wanted one, that much was clear, but I didn't want to be halfway through the process if it suddenly became go time. God forbid I should drop any . . . the thought alone sent a shiver up my spine. I decided to give it another few minutes, see if anything popped off.

Being patient was not my strong suit, I decided, as I fished out the packet of rolling papers.

I was so focused on my task, grinding, filling, and rolling, that I didn't even notice that there was more than one source of music now reaching my ears. If Johnny hadn't stopped playing, leaving that second fiddle to be the sole source of sound, I would've likely not noticed at all.

But when that second fiddle reached my ears, without Johnny's playing to mute it, my head shot up. It was . . . *beautiful.* Like, it took my fucking breath away, it was so beautiful. Johnny was good, likely about the best I'd ever heard until *this* came along. This was something else entirely. Now I knew just what he meant and got a sense for what he'd been looking for. And hearing those notes, I wanted it for him, too, if only so it meant I might get to hear it more often myself.

I crammed my weed paraphernalia into the little shopping bag I'd been carrying, making damn sure not to spill anything. It was a near thing, as my hands were shaking with excitement, but I got the green where it needed to be. Digging into my front pocket, I pulled out a tiny baggie of coke and instantly snorted it. Then I licked the bag clean, rubbing the last little remnants onto my gums. I wanted to be amped right the fuck up, just in case. Never knew when a little extra juice might come in handy.

Johnny was looking at me, and I nodded. "Yeah, let's do this," I muttered around my tongue, sucking my few remaining teeth.

Wet set off at a trot through the woods, skirting the creek as we went. The music grew steadily clearer, louder, as we jogged, letting us know we were getting ever closer. I was going to take the lead, but I decided to let Johnny go first. My sense of self-preservation was high—higher than my sense of what was right—and I mean, technically I was hired to make contact and get him lessons, not keep him safe. Sure, it might've been implied . . . but like the devil, I was a stickler for the details if ever doing so was to my benefit.

I wasn't proud of that stance. But it was what it was. Maybe one day I would be better, I thought, but for now I was just angling to make sure I stayed alive long enough to finish off these drugs I had bought. A man has to have priorities.

After three or so minutes of jogging, I was pretty winded. Not because I didn't have any endurance or anything, but more from being a heavy smoker. I was regretting every step that had led me to that moment; my lungs were burning, and I was wheezing like a train smokestack. I was so caught up in my breath that this time I *did* run into Johnny when he stopped. I smacked right into the back of him—pretty hard, in fact, which sent us both sprawling. My bag of goodies flew one way and his fiddle flew another, and I don't know which of us cried out louder at that fact. It was a near thing, that much was sure.

I looked up as I started to scramble to my feet, and what I saw caught me up short. Not so short that I didn't keep my hands reaching and grabbing to try and find my drugs, but it certainly kept my eyes looking up. And looking up wide.

The creek was dammed across its width by a beaver dam. You could clearly see where the vermin had been chewing the lengths of wood and piling them up. It was made a knotty tangle of limbs that rose about four feet up from the surface of the creek, and it looked to be wide enough that you could walk across it, if you felt lucky. I'd seen too many cottonmouths in dams over the years to try it, but the option was there for the foolish, I reckoned.

Beyond that, the creek widened out into what wasn't big enough to call a full pond, but something a little more than a creek. It was an expanse of water maybe forty feet wide at the broadest point, and it went back farther than I could easily see. Trees grew up throughout it, most of which had died and were rotting away or had been ringed out by the beavers so that they were steadily dying. Snarls of stumps jutted up like jagged teeth throughout, and the water was more green than brown, being covered with a thick, stagnant algae.

And there, in the middle of it all on a broken stump, fiddle in hand, sat the creature.

It was hard to tell just how tall it was, seeing as it was not only seated, but much of it below the knee was obscured under the water. I could tell, though, that it was easily taller than either of us. With me that was no great feat, but Johnny was obnoxiously tall to go along with being obnoxiously good-looking.

Its skin was green, almost the exact same shade as the algae, though perhaps just a tiny little bit more pale. Its head was wider than a humans, though the same shape, with giant eyes that looked like dingy gold coins. They were set in a noseless face, above a broad mouth spreading in a smile that revealed an uncomfortable number of sharp-looking teeth.

It was all weird, of course, but the cherry on top? The damn thing was dressed in what looked like its Sunday best. It had on a pair of nice dark slacks that were rolled up to just below the knee, keeping them dry. A white button-up was tucked into it, with a slim black tie hanging loosely around the thing's neck. A silver tie pin held it in place, though at this distance I couldn't see exactly what it was shaped like.

In its hand it held a violin. I was no violinist, or any sort of musician at all, but it looked pricey. The wood was dark and had a sort of greenish tinge to its edges. It shone with a nice polish, and the little knobby bits you'd use to tune it looked like they were made of brass. They'd taken on that sorta greenish patina that old brass gets, which I always found to be mighty attractive as I pawned it. The bow, sliding to and fro across the strings, was carved from the same dark wood as the violin, with what looked like some pearl insert at the handle. It was a thing of beauty.

Beside me, Johnny slumped to the ground.

INTERLUDE: TAKE US BACK, OH TAKE US BACK

"Why did you stop?" Cross asked crossly.

I giggled at that thought, trying to convince myself immediately after that it didn't sound nervous or panicked at all. "I'm hungry, and more than a little parched. If I'm at risk of soul sucking and such, I want a good meal in me. And I'm gonna need something to drink if you want me to keep telling my story."

Not only had I stopped telling the story—I had pulled the car into the parking lot of a little restaurant set back off the road beneath a trio of Spanish-moss-laden trees. I didn't much care what kind of food they had on offer, as I was more thirsty than hungry, but I figured maybe something would shake loose and I could work out some sort of escape plan. Driving inside a locked-up car wasn't the move; I knew that much.

The devil nodded after a moment. "Let's be quick about it."

A couple minutes later the three of us were sitting in a booth, each with a slightly sticky menu in hand. It was your typical Southern style dinner, and being a classy location, they had Coke instead of Pepsi. That was really the most important thing. If I was gonna die, I didn't want to die with a bladder full of rancid sugar water. I wanted something worth a fuck.

"Don't suppose you're gonna be treatin' us to lunch?" I asked Cross.

He stared at me for a moment, then gave that creepy "leaves on pavement" laugh of his. "I love the audacity."

"So's that a yes?" I ignored Jackie-O's wide eyes staring at me from the seat next to me.

Cross, still chuckling, flagged down a passing waiter. He was a tired-looking man with sweat stains around the armpits of his faded blue work shirt. "Whatever these two want, put it on my bill."

"Hell yeah," I said, with a surprising amount of excitement. I mean, the guy was very likely about to kill us, but fuck, I did love getting free food. Especially when I didn't have to kick my annoyance factor into overdrive to get it.

You might think that I would avoid being my usual extra self in this instance, in a dedicated effort to not piss off the devil sitting across from me. I regret to inform you that if you are, you haven't really been paying too much attention to me. Besides the biggest Coke they had on offer, I got an order of fried pickles to start, a chicken fried steak with fried okra, coleslaw, and cornbread for the main course, a double bacon cheeseburger to go, an extra side of fries, and three slices of pie, one each of what they had on offer. Jackie got a hot dog with chips to go with his glass of water.

Goddamn mooching amateur hour.

"I ain't sharing with you," I said to him sternly when he got done ordering.

"I ain't asking," he hissed back. There was a window by our booth, slightly offset so that you couldn't get a great view out of it from our side of the table. That didn't stop Jack from staring out it, no doubt wishing he was anywhere else in all the world. Not that I blamed him, but if a frog had pockets, he'd carry a pistol and wouldn't worry about snakes.

"Nothing for me, thanks," Cross said to the waiter, handing over his menu. Grinning savagely, he looked dead at me and softly added, "I'm saving room for later."

I suddenly wasn't as hungry as I had been. I had faith it would come back by the time the food got served, though. I'm an optimist like that sometimes.

"You can continue the tale now," Cross said, leaning back in the booth as he did so.

I took a long sip of tea. It was cold, and the few teeth I got, it may surprise you to learn, aren't exactly the best cared for. So I had to go slow with it, taking care to not trigger some pain. I was mostly successful in that, which also gave me a little thinking time.

"I reckon I'll pick the story back up when we get in the car. How's that sound? I don't like to talk around a mouth full of food and such. 'Sides, I feel like we hardly know you at all, Mr. Cross. Why don't you tell us 'bout what takes you to Drew?"

"No."

"No?" About then I felt Jack shift a little, and felt his shoe collide with my leg. I didn't know if he was a clumsy shit or if he was trying to keep me quiet and complacent, but he just had to learn to trust me. Not like I had given him any reason not to so far—I mean, not really. I pulled my leg under me where he couldn't get at it.

"You are here for my amusement, not the other way around. And I won't give you anything you might could use against me, so stop fishing."

"I mean, technically we're here 'cause I got hungry. That, and you sorta hijacked us. We'd be most of the way to NOLA by now 'cept for you. "

That brought a sour smile to his grim face. "Going to go visit dear Uncle Rooster Marsh, no doubt. He and I go way back. Did you know that?"

I hate pretty much all of my family save three: Krista, Hubert Dale, and Rooster. And Rooster mostly got a pass because he lived well the fuck off from the rest of us and wasn't nearly as uptight as most of the others. He might have been a righteous toolbag these days, for all I knew, but last time I'd seen him, we'd done a fat rail together and spent the night in some shitty Montgomery bar. It'd been a good time all around.

So to hear this devil imply what he was implying, well, it kinda cut me to the quick. Rooster's relative success compared to the rest of my family suddenly took on a whole new light.

Unless Cross was fucking with me. You can never trust any sort of demon, as they'll say anything to get under your craw. It would explain, though, why I was already on this fucker's radar. 'Cause let's be real—I ain't the sort of person you go out of your way to notice. Not unless you have an especially tempting bit of loose valuables lying around unattended.

"How'd you two meet?" I asked, hoping he was full of shit.

Cross just grinned, sharklike. "Let's just say that if you rummage through my guitar case here, one of the cassettes might have a bit of tape with your uncle's name on it."

"The cassettes are souls?" Jack asked, horror creeping into his voice.

"Let me be clear—they tend to take the form of whatever is nearest that will play them. It's been a long time since they were cassettes. These days, they are almost always CDs. Used to be they were seven-inch vinyl, and before that, they were sheet music. I do miss the vinyl, but cassettes . . . meh. If I'd known your car had a tape deck, I might have rethought it all," Cross laughed.

I'd known that guitar case was magic the moment he'd whipped out his guitar, but that each of those represented a soul . . . there had been scores upon scores of cassettes in there. I felt sick to my stomach. And the thought of Rooster's soul being in there, too . . . it didn't bear thinking about. I didn't have the first clue about how I might try and get it up outta there, and if that would even do any good, but I knew I was gonna have to try.

Goddamn, I hated having a conscience.

I wasn't about to let Cross know the effect he was having on me, though.

"You actually gave Rooster something of value for his soul?" I made that sort of face that said "Well *that* wasn't a choice I would have made." And too be fair, Rooster wasn't a whole lot better off than me in a lot of regards, which is probably why we got along as well as we did. "Hell, the way he churns through hookers and blow, I reckon you'd have gotten it for free iff'n you'd been patient."

"Let your hair down, baby, we ain't gettin to heaven no ways," muttered Jack from beside me.

Cross's eyes widened just a fraction. "Slim Harpo! You do know your bluesmen. He's not one of mine, mind you—he'd be a bit more famous if he was. Still, I'm a little impressed. Not many these days could quote a Harpo lyric my way. And you aren't terrible on guitar. Not good enough to get anywhere with it, but maybe with a little help . . ."

The devil reached under the table and a heartbeat later pulled out a sheet of paper. "I prefer to conduct business a little more remotely, like in a graveyard or some forgotten little crossroads, but you have to strike while the iron is hot, as they say."

Even I laughed a little as Jackie-O damn near crawled over the back of the booth trying to get away from that contract. If I hadn't put a hand on his shoulder, I think the fool would've tried breaking a window or something equally dumb. Cross burst out laughing fit to be tied, so much so that he was actually crying. He used the contract to blot at the bloody tears that were starting to roll down his face, which I'll admit pretty well stopped my laughing.

"Now, then," Cross said, the last bit of chuckling dying on his breath. "Carry on, Mr. Marsh. You don't want to leave me waiting."

So I did.

Story Time with Howard Marsh: It's Been Real

Years Ago

The nacken nodded in our direction, never stopping its playing as it did so. I didn't want to take my eyes off it, but I also felt I needed to take a look at Johnny. So, risking a quick glance down, I saw that the man hadn't passed out like I had initially thought; he'd instead fallen to his knees. His eyes were wide and his jaw was flopping like a catfish in the bottom of jon boat. His fiddle was held loosely in his hands, and I was pretty sure he was going to drop it at any second.

"It's real," I heard him whisper.

I guess that's to be expected. It's one thing to be told something is real and to believe in it, maybe even hear it. But to see it in the flesh? It's a whole other sort of deal when you suddenly learn for a fact that creatures of lore and legend do actually exist. There was no way that you could look at this critter and think it was anything other than a thing of magic.

While not exactly calling up my power, I did get it ready to be drawn upon. It wasn't making any danger-ous moves—not yet, at least—and Uncle HD had said it wasn't dangerous, probably, but it didn't hurt to be a little cautious. For all I knew, it was trying to bespell us with music. It didn't feel like it, though, beyond the whole "being the most beautiful music I've ever heard in my life" thing.

I feel like I'm underselling that—I was legit crying with-out even realizing it. Not being quite the music man that Johnny was, I don't think it hit me quite as hard, but I ain't lying, it was sorta life-changing. The tune was soaring, not happy, not sad, just . . . epic. It was otherworldly, and every note painted a picture of times and places no human had ever set foot in or on. When the first notes had come, they had been sorta riffing on what whatever Johnny played. Now that it was solo, with every passing moment it slowly shifted into a song of elsewhere.

I'd never heard something like the likes of this, and I wasn't about to do anything to risk that song stopping. Unless it started making us walk into the water . . . then I'd attempt to stop it. Maybe. I'd feel bad about it, though.

"How . . . ?" Johnny whispered.

"You ain't hallucinating, if that's what you're wondering. And I'm the only one high as a kite," I said, my voice kept low enough that only he could hear me, hopefully. I was surprised to hear that my words flowed in tune with the music. It was like I was doing some sort of spoken word singing along with the music, and it made my common words feel a little more heard, if that makes any sense. Like I was some sort of prophet or bard telling some legendary story, not a half-baked wizard talking about being ripped on blow.

Johnny looked at me, then back to the nacken, who was still smiling and playing. Those teeth were sharp looking, sure, but the smile was warm and welcoming. Which, knowing fae critters, it was probably fifty-fifty if this was some sort of trap. If someone was gonna get bit, well, I reckoned it would be the idiot at my side since I was keeping at least some sense about myself, I thought.

Climbing to his feet, Johnny thankfully managed to not drop his fiddle. He didn't try to play; he was fool enough to want to learn from the fae, but not fool enough to think that his playing could come close to comparing to what the green-skinned beastie in front of us was whipping up. At least, that's how it seemed to me. He was also smart enough to not get any closer now that he had regained his footing.

"Can you teach me?" Johnny asked, his voice so soft that I could barely hear him even though I was right by him. Fae had good ears, but I had my doubts they were *that* good, what with the music playing. I did note that his words were said in tune to the music.

I sorta gave him a little elbow. "Say it with your chest, boy," I said, giving my best high school football coach impression.

"Can you teach me?!" he shouted in a gross overcorrection. I flinched, and so did he. He coupled his flinch with his free hand rising to cover his mouth. I'd have felt bad for him, but I was kinda getting a little annoyed. This was really eatin' into my day, and he needed to get the ball rolling, get things set up for the future so as I could get him to take me back to my trailer.

That, and pay me.

For a moment I sorta thought about the implications. Here I was, taking an utter novice in the supernatural world of fairy bullshit, and I was about to just turn him loose with a creature that I didn't really have any sort of understanding of—just leave 'em totally unsupervised and let whatever happens, happen. It's not like I had a playbook of how this sort of shit was supposed to go, but I was pretty sure if there was, this wasn't in there. Dealing with creatures like this was almost always dangerous in some way.

I decided I didn't care. Johnny was a grown-ass man, and I'd done what he asked. He was in front of the critter he'd wanted me to help him find, so my work was basically done. If it went bad for him, well, I reckoned he would think a little harder before he asked for some dumb shit next time. Some lessons, you learned the hard way, and I didn't have the inclination to help soften that blow.

On its stump, the nacken grinned.

It was a nasty-looking smile.

Interlude: I've Sinned All of My Life

"Jaysus . . ." Jackie-O muttered.

I rolled my eyes at the interruption. "Soundin' pretty judgy there, cuz."

"Soundin' pretty shitty there, cuz," he spat back at me.

He wasn't wrong. I ain't no kinda saint, not by a long stretch, but who I am today is a far sight different from who I was back then. Well, maybe not a far sight. I mean, drugs ruled me then and they rule me now, so that's the same. But back then they did a better job of dulling that little bit of nagging conscience that I sometimes failed to keep tamped down these days.

"I don't see anything wrong," Cross said. "People make choices, usually bad ones. Nothing strange about that."

"When the soul-stealing demon is on your side, maybe you should examine your life choices." Jack was pissed, but to be fair he'd basically been pissed since before we picked Cross up. It was hard to tell if anything had really changed.

"Do we want to hear the story, or do we want to sit around jaw-jackin' about the moral standing of Jubal County's most notorious druggie?" In truth, I'd have been fine with that. It'd be a quick conversation: there was none. But it would drag things out a bit, and maybe by then the food would have showed up.

"No. Let he who is without sin cast the first stone and all that," Cross said, looking knowingly at my cousin. It was a loaded stare, and I didn't really want to know what that was all about. Judging from the little squeak Jackie-O let out, neither did he. Cross turned his gaze back to me. "Carry on."

So I did.

Story Time with Howard Marsh: Gimme Three Steps

Years Ago

"You have skill," the creature said. It slowed its playing down and made it a good bit more quiet somehow. Magic, no doubt. It was easier to focus on the thing's words now. "Enough that I could perhaps teach you a few small items."

Johnny lowered his hand. "I would appreciate that. A lot." He'd managed to get his voice under control, I was pleased to hear.

"There is a matter of payment to be discussed first, of course," it said, slipping from the stump.

Even though the water was dark, I could see its legs working back and forth slowly beneath the surface. It sunk not one inch further into the water, but I could tell it wasn't because its feet were on the bottom. No, it was keeping itself afloat in what should have been an impossible manner by slowly kicking its feet to and fro. Gradually, it started to come closer, the bow never stopping as it crossed the strings of its incredible violin.

"I . . . uh . . ." Johnny fumbled his free hand to his back pocket, producing a worn leather wallet with an Alabama football *A* on it in faded crimson. "I got some money—I can pay. Just tell me how much."

The nacken stopped at the edge of the water. Now it stood on the soggy bottom of the beaver pond, little puffs of silty mud billowing around its toes as its feet sunk slowly down. The music shifted a little, becoming slightly more strident. It was letting it be known how insulting it was to offer a faerie creature money, if Johnny was smart enough to listen. "And what would I spend that money on out here in the swamp?"

As the sort of guy that no one was racing to add to their list of beautiful people, I will own that it sorta made my day to see someone like Johnny be so out of sorts. I don't mean he had life handed to him on a platter 'cause of those looks or anything; he lived in Jubal County, same as the rest of us, and no one in the County really had that easy a go of things. But it's sure harder on us ugly, less charming folks, so this whole thing was scratching an itch I didn't really know I'd had. I'd have felt worse about it, but . . . fuck 'em.

"Um . . . ah . . ." Johnny's mouth worked uselessly. He looked over at me, panic in his eyes. He wanted help, but he was looking in the wrong direction for that. I didn't have a damn clue what this thing might want, and I wasn't about to start guessing.

"The traditional payment is three drops of blood," crooned the creature.

Johnny looked back at me.

Anything to do with fairy folk and threes was generally not a good thing; I knew that much. Well, I take that back—they liked to work in threes, and most of their work was made with no nevermind toward us humans. You could use it to your advantage iff'n you were smart enough. And I rarely was, so I just tried avoiding them as much as possible. But this . . . I wasn't real jived on it. I tried to show it in my face, making a sour look.

"Will that . . ." Johnny sorta made this circling motion with one hand, like he was trying to summon up the words he needed from thin air. This was all a foreign concept to him, I reckoned, but he'd clearly heard enough folktales to have the gist of things. When the words didn't appear on his tongue, he started over. "What do I get for that?"

The nacken did a slow, lazy pirouette there in the water. His song shifted, and there was an age and weight to the music now. It spoke wordlessly of ancient pacts and long-held vows. Don't ask me how it did that, but I suddenly felt the heady weight of years come down on my shoulders, and for a moment I swear I saw, for the first time ever, the full scope of that secret world beyond the veil. It took my breath away.

As it spun, the creature gave voice to a small poem, said in time to the music.

"By one aligned,

Two entwined,

Three will bind."

With the words complete, it slowly swooped back into place before us, resuming its place in the mud. "Each drop will connect us, and allow us a sharing of the mind. It will ensure there is no falsehood between us, and will speed the learning."

"And how long will that last?" I asked incredulously.

The nacken looked at me, tilting its head. It occurred to me that I hadn't seen those overlarge golden eyes blink, not even once. "Until the lesson is complete. I have no desire to remain connected to a mortal overlong. But the occasional taste . . ." It gave a shrug, then shifted its song once again.

The notes now were sorrowful. There was a real sadness to them that was damn near soul-crushing. It was like the tune had buried its way into my chest, right down to my heart, and gouged a hole in it, spilling out every tear I'd ever shed. It was like every heartbreak being all ripped back open at once, every loss being relieved.

". . . it reminds me of what it's like to feel. To fear. You short-lived creatures, you feel so strongly! And the best music comes from a place of passion, or loss." It changed its song again, so fluidly that I only realized it when the crushing of my soul relented. It was like I could breathe again, and I actually staggered a half step. Johnny was full-blown sobbing. I guess he wasn't as numbed up on drugs as me. "So for as long as you study with me, we will be bound. Then I will break the ties that bind."

"But we only have your word that you'll release him. And no offense, but I done been burned by your kind once or twice. Y'all ain't the most trustworthy at times."

I love saying "no offense" when I'm specifically trying to be offensive. It's the little pleasures.

Johnny's jaw tightened, and he cut me one of those silent yet loud "Dude, shut the fuck up" sort of looks. But I mostly ignored him; I was really watching the nacken. I wanted to see its next move. To see what sort of offense it took, so I could see if I needed to start running. But I'll be damned, it didn't take any. 'Least the music didn't change, which I was learning was probably the best way to judge where this thing's head was at.

"It is of no matter to me. Pay, or leave; I am content either way. But for that insult, the price is now doubled. You must both pay. I want to taste the life of a man so bitter and burned as you."

Fuck.

Story Time with Howard Marsh: You Can Set My House on Fire, Baby

"That's gonna be a no from me," I said quickly. I had less than zero desire to be caught up any deeper in this mess than I had to be.

The nacken began to wend its way back out toward the center of the little beaver pond. The music didn't change, and it didn't even bother to shrug its shoulders with disappointment. "As I said, it doesn't matter to me. I am content."

"Excuse us a minute," Johnny said. Then he, no shit, gave a little, like, half bow. It was the damnedest thing. Fucking creature had its back to us when he did it, so the stupid thing didn't even see it.

I allowed him to grab my elbow and sort of guide me back away from the nacken. He did it with a soft touch, and broadly speaking, he was taking me in the direction I wanted to be heading anyway. I was of no mind to pay this thing what it wanted, so it was up to him to convince the critter that his blood alone was enough. Heading back toward the car seemed like the move for me.

"Help me out here . . . this is what I'm paying you for," Johnny said, keeping his voice low.

"Nope," I said, raising my hands, palms out. "I got you to the thing, and it's agreed to give you a lesson. It's on you to figure out payment. But I ain't on the menu."

"It's trying to eat us?" the tall man asked, his eyes wide.

I wanted to groan. "No, it was just an expression. But point is, we only got its word for what it wants, and what it wants it for. Creatures like that, they lie as easy as breathing. I ain't a fool, so I ain't paying. You want to pay, you can. But don't come crying to me if shit goes sideways."

Johnny straightened from where he had been leaning in my direction. He looked back to the creature, which had reclaimed its spot on the stump. It had never stopped playing, and maybe it was having more of an effect on me than I knew, 'cause my temper was fraying but still holding together mostly. Usually I'd have done been stalked off, throwing up a pair of birds as I shifted my shit-kickers on outta there. It was some damn pretty music, and honestly, I coulda listened to it all day.

"Then I'm not paying."

"That's between you and it," I said, sorta surprised he was being sensible.

"No," he said, turning his head back to face me. "I'm not going to pay *you*. Deal was, we get me a lesson, and since you won't play ball, our business is done."

"Look here, you little shit," I started. That music could only do so much to calm me down, and my control was getting lost in a haze of cocaine-fueled energy and a sudden spike of anger.

"I said my piece. But to meet you partway, I'll pay you an extra fifty bucks per drop of blood. Best I can do, and I'm not negotiating any more."

I was a man of two souls at that moment. There was that ornery, indignant side of me that was fully prepared to tell him to kick rocks and suck my dick. But on the other side . . . well, a hundred and fifty bucks was a shit ton of money for my broke ass. Hell, maybe I could even slip it to my asshole landlord to buy me a little time, I lied to myself.

"Are the drugs worth risking my life?" I asked myself, foolishly. Immediately, I'd started thinking of all the extra goodies I was gonna buy. But I had to salvage a tiny snippet of pride.

"Call it two hundred extra and the damn thing can suck my toes for all I care."

Story Time with Howard Marsh: The Dirty Money That You Earn

Years Ago

T he neck thing had come back over to the shoreline, standing there expectantly. He was still playing, an idle tune that lacked a little bit of its earlier majesty, as clearly the thing's focus was less on the music now and more on us. I kept watch for any signs that this thing was a little too eager, but either it was a much cooler cucumber than I could manage, or it hadn't been lying.

Or perhaps it knew it had us over a barrel, and that humans are pretty much collectively as smart as a box of hammers. I knew I was feeling real stupid, but I was gonna cry myself to sleep in a few days when I finally came down from all the drugs I was gonna buy. Every bit of this was stupid, especially on my account, because I knew just how tricksy these fucks usually were. But . . . I found I didn't care. I wanted that extra money to go with the money I'd already been promised. It was dumb greed, plain and simple, and I didn't really care. I should have. But I didn't.

I didn't have much of a life worth livin' no ways.

"How we doing this, then?" Johnny asked. He had a buck knife in his hand that he'd taken from one of his pockets. The blade was out and he was holding it near his other hand, ready to make a cut, from the looks of it.

"Nick your hand, then drip three drops onto my tongue," the neck said. It squatted down, taking care to not get its pants in the water. It was an awkward pose, which sorta soothed me in a weird way 'cause fey critters, they were usually so graceful and polished. To see one doing this sort of odd half-squat, half-hunch move—it was anything but regal.

Johnny flinched a little as he dug his knife into the tip of his index finger. I saw blood start to well up from the small hole, a splotch of crimson against his well-calloused hands. Then he reached out and hovered the hand over the open mouth of the neck.

There were a whole lot of teeth just a couple inches from his hand. I couldn't get the mental image of that thing just going full shark and chomping that hand clean off—but the critter only stuck out its tongue. It was broad and flat, with a color like liver. Then Johnny squeezed, and the drops fell. *One, two, three.*

The neck closed its mouth and eyes, and I could see it was moving its tongue around inside its mouth. It was like some sort of blood sommelier, checking the vintage on Johnny's offering. A small moan of pleasure escaped its lips, and it smacked its mouth indolently. Straightening, it opened its eyes once again. "Mmm, you do have some small skills. Very nice. Very nice."

Its music shifted, starting to play a song that was a lot more like the fiddle playing I was used to hearing. This was old-style bluegrass, like what came down out the mountains by the hands of Bill Monroe.

Johnny handed me the knife, blade open, almost as an afterthought. He didn't even try to stop the bleeding in his finger; instead, he scooped up his fiddle and joined in. Clearly, he knew the song even if I didn't, and within a heartbeat they were playing as one. The neck was still more skilled of course, and it shifted to let Johnny take the main melody. Then it began to play around him, expanding and toying with the tune. You could damn near taste the mountains through that music.

The two of them began to speed up a little, the neck . . . seemingly pulling Johnny along somehow? There was no question who was in charge, and even though Johnny was playing the main melody, it was the creature that set the pace. I ain't no sort of musician, but even I was impressed at the skill being whipped out before me. I wasn't sure if Johnny was better than I'd thought, or if the lessons were already starting and the neck was giving him what he paid for.

As they played, the neck turned to face me. Its look was expectant, and it suddenly became a lot more real. I gazed down at the knife in my hand and the cold hand of fear gripped my heart. I was fucking up, but I'd already passed the point of no return. Their fiddles were singing together, and Johnny had already made his half of the payment.

Creatures like this could, and frequently would, lie and cheat to get what they wanted. But there was absolutely no doubt as to what happened if you tried to welch on a payment: they would respond with as much violence as they could muster. You did not, under any circumstance, refuse a promised payment. 'Least not if you wanted to keep your life.

I looked back to the nacken. Its eyes had gone hard, as if it could read my mind already and knew I was having second thoughts. It began to lead the tune in a more . . . threatening direction. I could hear the hints of it in the odd strident note, and I knew the longer I took, the more tumultuous that music would get. And if it hit its point of no return? I'd probably die right here.

Gripping the knife tightly, I knew I had to make a choice right then: pay, or strike first. Only by killing the thing before it had a chance to use its power on me could I be likely to live. I could probably have done it, too, if I wasn't a such a coward.

I dug the tip of the blade into the tip of my thumb. It hurt like hell, but I made a point of not flinching. My eye may have twitched a little, but I don't think it could've seen that, looking down like I was. I needed this thing to know I was a hard motherfucker, not to be messed with. Because I didn't know what was coming next, and I wanted it to have at least a little bit of respect for me.

Which, considering it was me, was kinda laughable, but a boy could dream.

The bow still working across the strings, the neck hunched down once more. I was much shorter than Johnny, and while the thing could have hunched to the same degree as before and just let my hand rise to meet its mouth, it managed to contort even more awkwardly, I guess to be obliging.

And you know what? That actually put my mind to rest a bit. Most fey, they were stiff-necked as all hell, pun intended. That one would actually try to be accommodating like that, well, it meant that this one was probably not as potentially evil as many of them could be. So, with my heart still beatin' pretty fast but my mind a nudge calmer, I stretched out my hand.

Squeezing my thumb against my curled fist, I got a fat drop of blood to well up. Below, the neck's fat tongue extended, spread wide to catch it. It fell, landing in a dab of crimson that was almost instantly absorbed by the damp expanse of pale pink flesh. It was followed quickly by two more as I squeezed. *One, two, three.* As the third drop hit, I shifted my hand back so no more could spill onto it.

The neck shuddered, a spastic twitch that was unlike anything it had done with Johnny's blood. As I looked, it licked its lips, smacking loudly. It shuddered again, like it was rebooting or something. It staggered then, taking a half step back. It caused the water to splash a little, which was the most I had seen it do so yet, and it soaked the rolled-up cuff of its pants.

Sure that shit had gone sideways, I started to back up myself. The neck straightened up, and I could see that its oversized eyes had somehow gotten even larger. It was blinking furiously like it had gotten something stuck in them. As I watched, I could see its eyes were starting to dilate.

"Fuck," I hissed. I hadn't thought about what effect all the drugs in my system might do to a creature like this. To be clear, I didn't have beginner levels of drugs coursing through my system, either—I was on some real shit, the kind that might well kill someone who hadn't built up the tolerances I had.

The music then went slap of the rails. Johnny, hit with the same amount of "what the fuck" as I was, had stopped playing, though he still had his instrument at the ready. He kept looking from me to the creature, his mouth gaping open, his eyes slightly narrowed in confusion. But the neck was still playing . . . well, sorta.

What notes were coming out weren't really a melody, at least not one that I think anyone human would recognize. It wasn't totally discordant, but there were a jumbled mess of weird notes spilling out next to each other. It was like it was playing the song with every note a half line off while still somehow managing to not sound a string of pure shrillness.

It took a step toward me, slowly, then another. For the first time it set foot on dry land, and I could see that its wide flat feet only had about three toes, and they were webbed at that. They weren't the feet of a land creature, that much was clear, which gave me hope I could outrun it if need be. Regardless, I finally managed to think clearly enough to start summoning up my power.

Those large, dilated pupils seemed locked onto my thumb. I had a guess that it wanted more, so I ducked that hand out of sight behind my back. When I did, the neck snarled and curled its lips back to show those twin rows of lethal-looking teeth. "Give it to me," it managed to say through clenched teeth, making the words sound even more needy and viscous.

It looked like it was getting ready to spring forward as it dropped its pristine fiddle and bow. I started getting ready to summon up some flame, praying that even though it was some sort of water creature that it could still burn. With my free hand I held that knife out, ready to use it if the damn thing came too close before I could cast my spell.

And then the neck squeaked. With a gasp, it fell forward, falling face-first into the earth. And then it didn't move any more.

"Fuck me . . . I killed it."

Interlude: Good News to You, I'll Tell

I was interrupted by the food arriving. It struck me as funny enough to laugh, as it took two of them to bring the food. Our waiter, sweating heavily, had my food arrayed carefully between his two hands, but it was enough to have him full up, so an elderly woman with kind eyes was bringing up the rear. Only she was just holding one lonely-looking plate with a sad little hotdog and a bag of Golden Flake chips.

Don't get me wrong—I love chips, and I will fuck up an all-beef frank in a heartbeat. But that pathetic little number looked like it was boiled, which was strike one, and had the look of a dog made from peckers and lips. It was a sickly-colored thing that was probably more chicken cast-offs than anything worth actually eating. And when you compared it to the feast that was set down before me, well, it looked all the more pitiful.

I ain't eatin' no dog that's boiled unless it turned the water pink in the process. Iff'n you're gonna go processed, I want to taste the artificial cancer-causing flavor—don't half-ass it. All beef, or all chemicals. Ain't no in-between in the Marsh household.

The best part was seeing Jackie just sorta collapse in on himself when that dog flopped down limply in front of him. Now that it was closer I could see the bun had a little age on it, at least in the parts where it wasn't soggy from hot dog water. The tiny little mustard packet on the side was just the cherry on top. As potential last meals went, well, I'd rather just go ahead and get on with the death part than choke down that bit of sorrow made flesh.

"Don't even so much as *look* at my plate," I said to my cousin, scooping up my silverware. "Plates, rather."

It was deep Southern fried goodness, and while I don't have a ton of reference points to world cuisine, I daresay there ain't nothing better. I started sawing into my country fried steak, and I could damn near feel my arteries already clogging. It was delightful.

"Can you not eat and talk at the same time?" Cross asked.

Popping a mouthful of fried meat into my mouth, I grinned big. I'm self-conscious as all hell about my teeth, but I had a point to make. I started carefully working at chewing with the few teeth I had left. It wasn't all that easy of a process, and judging from the sour look on the devil's face, I had gotten my point across.

"Point made."

And so we ate mostly in silence, other than the sound of Cross tapping his fingers impatiently on his guitar case. I was pretty sure he was tapping out some tune; it had that kind of cohesive sound, but I wasn't sure what it was. Honestly, I probably didn't want to, so I just focused on tucking into the grub, which was as glorious as greasy spoon Southern food can be.

Jackie-O finished his dog in a rush, which was a fool move. With that and the chips done, he had nothing to do but just sit there awkwardly as I kept eating. The one time his hand started to drift in the direction of my food, I paused, fork halfway to mouth, and cut him a look. He played it off like he was just reaching for a napkin, but I knew better. And the look I gave him made him think better of it.

And so I was able to eat my fill in peace. I'll be honest, I sorta made a pig of myself, but I had zero regrets 'cause you see, it gave me an idea on how we just might get out of this alive.

Setting my fork down, I pawed at my face with a napkin. I'd need a box to hold my leftovers, a fair-sized one, but

I had made sure to save room for my pie. As the waiter passed by, I waved him down. "I reckon I'm ready for that pie now. And I'll need a box."

"Jaysus," swore Jackie-O.

"While we wait, I reckon I can carry on. That make you happy?" I asked Cross.

He arched an eyebrow.

"Aight, then . . ."

Story Time with Howard Marsh: Down in the Gully

Years Ago

"What the fuck!?" Johnny shouted. His voice was pitchy, damn near a shriek.

Which sure fit what I was feeling. I knew I was damn near poison to be around, but I didn't think that was fucking *literal.* I was gabbling something back at him, but I couldn't tell you what I was saying; I was too busy being on the verge of a total come apart myself.

I was wrangling with just setting the damn thing on fire, to be on the safe side, or just hightailing it on out of there. Johnny was in a full-blown freak-out, kindly oscillating between shouting at me and shouting at the dead body in front of us. Not that I blamed him, even if the louder he got, the more I wanted to add a third option of lighting him on fire. Not that I would. Probably.

Settling on a middle ground of doing nothing, I started shouting back at Johnny. It was real important to my pride that I make it abundantly clear that this was all his fault—how I hadn't wanted to give the fucking thing my blood anyway, that was all his doing.

It probably wasn't the best moment to bring up the fact I still expected to be paid. But then when is it ever a good time to talk money, right? Twenty seconds of a lesson was still a lesson, I reckoned, and I had given my blood, so that was that. He needed to pay me. So I was just tryin' to make that clear, even though he was currently being a bit irrational. He'd come around.

Things started to escalate a bit when we started getting in each other's face. Johnny sorta tapped my chest with his fiddle bow, which made me a lot more pissed than it probably should have, but that was the wonder of drugs. I was working up a real coke rage, and he was about two steps from entering a world of fucking hurt.

"Son, if you so much as *dream* of tapping me with that stick again, you best wake the fuck up and apologize!" I shouted.

Then the motherfucker did it again. On purpose. With *malice.* That bow flicked out and hit my sternum, and I knew it was gonna be on like Donkey Kong. I dropped that knife before I did something stupid, then started to whip my shirt off, as you do right before throwin' down.

My shirt hit the ground about the same time as the neck stood back up. Damn thing rose straight up like some old-timey vampire in the black-and-white movies coming up out the coffin. I don't know what was louder: my shriek, Johnny's shriek, or the neck making this sort of gurgly roar.

Its eyes were so dilated, they looked as though they were damn near solid black. The parts that weren't pure pupil were a spider web of bloodshot veins, and it may as well have not had eyelids for all it blinked. Spilling out over its bottom lip was a pink-tinged foam, like it had turned rabid. The pink would be blood, but whether it was internal or from it biting its tongue, I couldn't tell.

Unfortunately, from having too many dead friends, I knew a bad OD when I saw one. This critter was a dead man walking; it just didn't know it yet.

Not that it slowed the fucker down.

I was already backing up, sorta half turning so I could book it outta there, the same time as I called up my power. "Get!" I yelled at Johnny, who looked frozen in fear.

The neck raised its waterlogged fiddle to its shoulder, I saw, and started to run its bow across the muddy strings. It made for a strident noise at first as the mud was slung from the strings, but after a couple of seconds pure music was flowing from it once again—only instead of the songs of wonder and glory it had been making earlier, it now loosed a hateful dirge on us.

Before I could get my flame spell off, my body became locked up. My mind still worked, but I could tell there was a real compulsion on it, some sort of geas no doubt enabled from my blood. Inside my mind I screamed, but nothing came out. Trying to thrash around but being unable to move so much as a muscle, well, that was a special sort of hell. I could still feel everything, though, from the humid touch of the air on my skin to the dampness soaking into my shoes from the muddy ground. I just had no control, and I wanted to scream more than life itself.

Then the music started to sink in. A bone-deep sorrow began to fill my soul, obscuring any attempt at real thought. My brain was a fog now of misery and tears as all the sorrow I'd ever felt in my life began to bubble up from the darkest corners of my mind. All I could focus on was the water of the small pond before me, how inviting those depths looked. If I could but fling myself in that cool embrace, I could free myself of all my worldly sorrows.

I began to take shuddering steps toward the water.

Story Time with Howard Marsh: Dying to Get You in the Palm of My Hands

Years Ago

I wasn't sure if it was the drugs messing with the normal flows of my brain or my innate magical ability, but it seemed like I was resisting a good bit better than Johnny was. While I was taking slow, hard-fought steps, he was strolling right along toward the water like he was on his way to a summer picnic. His hands opened and his fiddle and bow fell to the ground, and before I knew it he was ankle-deep.

I wasn't sure what the critter had planned for once we were in there, but I was damn sure it wasn't good. Being, you know, human, we were buoyant, so it wasn't like it could drown us just by having us walk in—I was pretty sure, at least. It must have been planning to pull or hold us under, I decided.

My mental struggle didn't let up, and I could tell it was having some effect. The neck was pretty much ignoring Johnny in favor of me. Those huge eyes were locked on me, and that foaming mouth churned into a bleak grimace filled with hate. The music started to change from pure sorrow to the anger of loss. It was the sort of painful song of someone mourning the death of someone who had died too young, too needlessly, and the feeling of fruitless anger cutting through the sadness.

It was a song I felt deep in my core.

I thought of the friends I'd lost. Belle Dennings, who last year had gotten fucked-up on pills and slit her wrists. Quevarious Johnson, who, my junior year, had gotten drunk as hell and wrapped his car around a tree after a field party. Billy Randall and Paul Herbert, who'd OD'd on the same bad batch of coke a couple years back. All them plus a half dozen more on top of that.

But strongest of all was the soul of that neck sobbing out at the futility of its own death. It knew it was dying, and for what? Because of its greed and my poison. Because some stupid mortal wanted to learn to play the fiddle better. In what world was that worth a life? The life of something that had lived for centuries, done magic that spanned two continents, and had so much more to give?

The sorrow I started to feel at that was real, and something outside the feelings the song was forcing on me. If I lived, I knew this was gonna be one of those things that haunted me.

If I lived.

I couldn't turn my eyes, which were starting to dry out and burn from the lack of blinking, but that didn't mean I couldn't see. The neck was full up in my line of sight so that I could see every move it made, even if my attention was mostly focused on that cool, inviting depth of murky green-brown water. That didn't stop me from seeing the instruments it was carrying begin to merge and blend into its flesh, vanishing before my very eyes. They were consumed by the creature's body but the music never stopped, never missed a note. If anything, it began to play faster, and I could feel my resistance start to slip a little bit.

Then I watched in horror as it began to shift its form.

It was a bizarre, horrifically grotesque sight—imagine a body getting turned inside out and stretched. I could hear the bones creak and groan until they snapped in a crackling thunder that filled its body. Its face stretched and elongated, its eyes being split wide and sliding to the side of its now much larger, longer visage. Its teeth remained just as sharp, but they now crowded into a mouth much closer to that of a horse than a man, forming a double row on both top and bottom.

The thing bray-screamed, a sound that was half horse, half man, and all terrible. It was pain made flesh, and it was letting us know it. The form kept shifting as it fell to all fours, its arms and legs lengthening. It was clear that it was shifting into a horse of some sort, but I had to think this wasn't normal. There was no way that any living creature would willingly go through a change so horrific.

I think the fear was clouding my mind a little, which, coupled with my natural magic/drug-fueled resistance, let me slow to damn near a crawl. I couldn't see Johnny anymore; he was off in the water somewhere, swimming out to the middle for all I could tell. Meanwhile, I had two eyes full of horror horse and was trying with all my might to break free so I could run the hell away. Johnny had made this mess; he could live or die with it without bringing me along for the ride.

The neck had fully changed now. Where there had once been a green-tinted man thing, there was now a tall gray-green horse. Its mane was stringy and thin, entwined with what looked like some sort of water lily. It wasn't a neat braid or nothing; instead, it had the look as though the vines were growing from it. It had an emaciated form so thin that I could see every bone jutting out from its wet hide. Rows of ribs, boney knobs at every joint, a skull-like visage . . . it was a thing of nightmares. There was no way any animal that looked that near death like that could be standing, yet it was.

The bloody foam still dripped from its mouth. It started to walk toward me, though it staggered more like a colt that had just been born. It could barely keep its hooves planted enough to stay standing, but somehow it made its way over to where I stood. All the while that horrible gallows song kept playing, coming from everywhere and nowhere all at once.

The tune changed a bit, and I didn't feel pulled toward the water anymore. My heart soared for a brief second, but then it came crashing right back down as I felt the tug filling my hands. I tried to fight it but my hands rose upwards, controlled by that unseen force. My arms were stretching out like I was some sort of Romero zombie extra, reaching out toward the neck.

The creature took another step, nudging its shoulder into my outstretched hands. I felt its clammy hide beneath my fingers, the gaunt muscle shifting beneath it. It was so thin I could feel the bone under that, hard and cold. It felt like death.

The song began to change again. The notes became more random sounding—the fluidity of the music was flowing away, no doubt chased off by the brain-shattering OD the beast was dying from. There was still a song there, buried under the misfiring neurons or whatever bullshit made up a fairy brain, but it was losing its cohesion.

I felt the compulsion leave my body. I was free to turn and run, and I jerked my body to do so but to my horror, my hands couldn't free themselves from the skin of the creature. It was like I was a rat caught in a glue trap, and I couldn't tear them free. I fought as hard as I could, yanking and pulling, but the harder I fought, the more of me that came in contact with the creature, and every part of me that touched it came just as stuck as my hands. Within a few seconds, pretty much my whole right arm was attached to the creature.

Then it started to walk into the water, dragging me right along with it.

Interlude: Nothing Quite as Good as Pie

The waiter set a Styrofoam box down on the empty space in front of Cross, then placed my pie before me. I was full as hell, but hear me now: it'll be a cold day in hell before I don't have room for pie. Three slices might have been excessive, though, even by my standards, so being the gracious sort that I am, I offered one to my cousin.

"No" was all he said—not even a "No, thanks for offering." I swear, some folks just weren't raised right, I reckoned. I mean, clearly me, but also other people.

I took that first mouthful of chocolate pie, and I swear my toes curled a little. There was some granny somewhere that was no doubt rolling over in her grave at her recipe having been stolen, because this was way too good to have been store-bought pie. It was so rich, I could damn near feel the diabetes setting in.

"Goddamn, that's good pie," I said. I scooped up a little bit on my fork and held it out across the table. "Cross, man, try this shit."

He arched an eyebrow, but didn't say anything. I shrugged and went back to eating, and generally living my best life. I might've been about to die, but at least I was going out with a belly full of the good stuff.

I sorta thought for a second about why I was suddenly in such a good mood. The threat of death was still there, but . . . I don't know. It didn't faze me as much now. Which got me to thinking hard, which, I'll admit, isn't my strong suit. I'm pretty smart for a guy whose life is one continuous bad decision, but self-inspection isn't a strong suit of mine.

But after thinking on it—I reckoned it was because of telling this story like I had been—I had come to realize something. I ain't of no account, not really. But back then? Back when all that shit went on with the neck? I was a real shit back then. The kind of person that current me wouldn't want to spend no time with. Which could have made me ashamed at what a bad person I'd been, but as I thought on it, I realized I was feeling good because while I wasn't anywhere near a stand-up guy now, I was a damn sight better than I was back then.

And *that* made me feel good.

It can be hard to see how far you've come without something to measure it against. I'd been doing a good job lately of trying to forget my worst deeds, so I'd needed something like this to cause me to put it all in perspective. There was no getting around it: Anna had been damn good for me. She was, just by being her amazing self, dragging me slowly upwards. Not so much as you'd notice in the course of a week, or a month, but I was consistently improving from who I'd been before I met her. It was enough to bring a tear to my eye, if I hadn't been so pie happy at the moment.

The other thing that had me feeling good was the fact that I'd started to get an idea of just how I could get out of this alive. The gears were churning, and it would just as likely blow up in my face as save me, but there's something to be said about being proactive. I mean, I actively try not to be as much as possible, but even a blind squirrel gets a nut sometimes.

Filling my mouth with another bite, I noticed that our damp waiter had set our check on the table but Cross had made no move to pick it up. I gestured toward it with my utensil. "You gonna get that?"

Cross glanced down as if noticing it for the first time. Instead of picking it up, he just snapped his fingers and the check burst into flames. It was nothing but ash in about two seconds flat, and I ain't gonna lie, it had me a little startled. Jackie-O, I thought, might have been on the brink of a total come apart.

"It's handled," the devil said, grinning wickedly.

"Fair enough," I said as calmly as I could muster. I still had a slice and a half of pie, as well as all my other leftovers. "On that note, Jackie, be a peach and box this shit up for me. I gotta rock a piss before we hit the road."

I slid out the booth and did my best to ignore the squawking that my cousin had started to loose in my direction. I really did have to use the bathroom, but I also wanted to try and see the lay of the land a bit if I could. That hint of a plan had formed but it was going to take some doing, and that, I hadn't really been able to think through fully. So, I was wildcattin' it, and if I wanted to make it out alive, well, I was gonna have to be smarter than I usually gave myself credit for.

I walked past Cross, heading toward the far side of the diner where there was a little sign for the bathrooms. Giving Dampness the Waitering a little nod as I passed by the register, I tried to put out my best "nothing to see here" vibes. Glancing back over my shoulder, I saw that Cross wasn't bothering to turn his head to watch me, so maybe they were working.

Rounding the long counter with its row of faded red bar stools, I passed the little waiter station with its rolls of tightly wrapped silverware, empty cups, and other sundries. It was unattended, and with no eyes on me that I could see, I scooped up what I needed and dropped it in my pocket. There was what looked like a money bag there as well—for their tips, no doubt—but I needed all the good karma I could muster, so I let it lie. Damn thing was probably empty anyways.

A few minutes later, I was done handling my business and made my way back to the booth. As expected, Jackie had not done what I'd asked, but that was fine. I settled back in and started putting my nibbles in the Styrofoam, trying to think happy thoughts about how good they would be later. I figured I would just keep telling myself there would *be* a later, sorta manifesting that fact into existence.

"You can box and talk at the same time," Cross said.

"How 'bout I finish up once we're in the car? I'll finish it then. We're gettin' near the end anyways. Pretty near it, least ways."

Cross sighed, but didn't say anything else. Could a demon have ADHD? If so, Cross sure enough had it the way he was carrying on. I just wrapped up the last of my food, taking care to set my pie where it wouldn't get contaminated by the rest of the food; I wanted it as pristine as possible. Nothing worse than getting gravy or the like on your pie.

That done, I pulled a set of wrapped up silverware from my pocket and sat it on top of my food, then closed the lid. "I hate a plastic fork," I said by way of explanation, not that anyone had asked.

Getting to my feet, I looked at my erstwhile road trip companions. "Well, what y'all waitin' on? Let's get."

INTERLUDE: TO KNOW YOU IS HARD, WE WONDER

I made a point of holding the door for Jack and Cross, letting them out into the bright light of day in front of me. I needed a nap after all that, if I was being honest. All that food had just 'bout put me in a food coma, and a little sleep was the cure for that. But I had be strong—I needed to be sharp, 'cause it was go time now.

There was only gonna be one shot at this, I reckoned, and if it didn't work out, I figured Cross would like as not suck the souls right outta us once we got him to where he wanted to go. So, with infinite care, I pulled my car keys from my pocket and waited for my time to strike.

Cross was heading for the back seat and Jackie-O went for the passenger seat, same spots as where we'd been when I'd pulled us in here not all that long ago. Cross was out front slightly, with Jack about two steps behind. My heart was pounding fit to bust, and I was glad the devil wasn't looking my way. I was sure I had to be showing some sign of the stress I was feeling.

When the devil placed his hand on the car door, I made my move. I took my keys and tossed them in Jackie's general direction. As I did, I said, "Fuck it, you drive."

Now, of course my cousin had his back turned to me, so he had no idea that I was even trying to toss him the keys. Which, in truth, I wasn't—in fact, I needed him to miss the keys. That was one of two integral parts of my plan.

The other half, which had my heart locked up in my throat so tight, I couldn't breathe, was that I needed those keys to land under the car. And not a little bit—I needed them to hit the ground and slide up right near the middle, far enough that they wouldn't be easy to reach, but not so far that they slid right out the other side.

I swear time slowed to a molasses-thick crawl. It was like a *Matrix* movie, where I could see every mote of dust swirling in the air. A white dove flew by in slow motion. In the background movie extras carried on, looking busy. Sunlight caught on the metal of the keys just right to bring them into focus. It was wild.

They hit the ground about a half a foot from the car, which was a little farther out than I had intended; I'm famed for my prodigious meth intake, not my manual dexterity and accuracy. When they landed, I was pretty sure I was boned.

There was one thing working in my favor, though: the fact that my key ring only had my car key and the key to my shed door. This was no heavy janitor-level ring chock-full of all sorts of shit, so they weren't too weighted down. The keys hit the asphalt with a slight jangle and started to slide. As they went under the car, I had to fight to not fist pump, and somehow I managed to keep my emotions in check. Besides, I was too close to see just how far under they had gone, so it was a little early to be celebrating.

"Fuckin' A," Jackie O said, turning to face me. "A little heads-up woulda been useful, jackass."

"Good catch, all-star," I spat back, putting a lot more heat on it than I actually felt.

Cross had stopped with the back door open, his hand on the top of it, just looking at us. Was there suspicion in his gaze? Or was I just being paranoid? I needed him to be inside the car so he couldn't see me. Standing there watching was exactly what I didn't need.

Jack and I had the same thought at the same time, and both of us leaned over to see where the keys had wound up. My heart soared to see they were almost exactly where I needed them to be. I would have liked them to be a little bit farther under, but it was clear that you couldn't just reach under and grab them. Someone was going to have to get down on the ground to snag them.

Straightening, Jackie shook his head. "I'm not getting those. You can crawl your happy ass under there."

Had I been purposely getting on my cousin's nerves for the whole meal just so he'd be extra contrary? Fuck no, I'm not that forward-thinking. But I certainly had accounted for it when I'd settled on my current course. Jackie was helpful, which was great, but I'd been pretty sure that I had him too riled up to be so currently. Which, in our current predicament, was playing out nicely.

I rolled my eyes for dramatic effect. "Fine, but you're still driving," I said, walking over to the side of the car. Cross was still standing there, though. He wasn't actually in my way, but he didn't know that, I reckoned. Looking him dead in the face, I made a little shooing motion with my hands. "You comin' or goin'?"

Cross stood there a moment longer, enough to make my heart skip a beat with worry. But in the end, he slipped inside the car and shut the door. That was my cue to get to work.

I got down on my knees, discovering that the asphalt was pretty damn hot. Hot enough it didn't feel real good, that was for sure, but there wasn't any other choice, so I got onto my belly, taking care to place my box of food where it wouldn't get stepped on. I could feel the noonday heat through my shirt, and fuck if it wasn't real unpleasant.

Edging forward, I reached my arm out, and with a snap I used the small magic that I used to tuck away small items for later use. Instead of my lighter, though, this time I whooshed up the large salt shaker I had snagged from the waiter stand. With my other hand, I unscrewed the top as quickly as I could. It was go time.

I ain't the praying type.

But today, I prayed.

Interlude: Jesus, Take the Wheel

"**J**ust hold it long enough for me to get us fucking going. Then you can set it up on the fucking dash," I told Jackie-O, my box of food thrust out in his general direction. I knew good and well that the moment I put it in drive, my food would go sliding off the dash, and I was not about to let this precious cargo go to waste. The fact that there were far bigger fish to fry in that moment didn't matter in the least, but my cousin was being real ass about it.

The fact that I was even driving was because he'd gotten a real burr in his bonnet about being asked to drive. My insistence that he "come down off the cross and use the wood to build a bridge to get the fuck over it" had, shockingly, gone over like a lead balloon. For a moment I wondered if this was what it was like to talk to me on the regular.

Begrudgingly, he finally took the box from me, holding it as I slipped the key into the ignition. I glanced back at Cross, who was sitting there real quiet-like with his guitar case between his legs. His look was expectant. "If you two are done squabbling, I want to hear the rest of the tale. You have me quite intrigued with this Johnny character—he would be a great addition to my case. Perhaps when my business in Drew is concluded, I might have to see about heading toward Jubal County."

That done stilled my heart. I hadn't even thought about the fact that a being like Cross would clearly be interested in someone like Johnny, what with his spark of power. It looked like at least three lives depended on my plan working now.

No pressure.

"Sure. Lemme just get rolling," I said, putting the car in drive. I knew I would find out in about two seconds if my plan had worked or not. And I wasn't really sure what might happen then . . .

I started to roll forward, and shit instantly hit the fan.

Cross slammed back in his seat with a gurgling cry. At the same time, my car's engine began to make a strained sound as we came to a dead halt. I was still pumping the gas, but we weren't going anywhere as the devil in the back seat began to strain and flail.

"What . . . did . . . you . . ." Cross managed to squeeze out between gritted teeth.

Beside me, Jackie had turned and was looking into the back seat, then back at me. "What the fuck?!" he was shouting, his voice reaching a flute-like pitch.

Ignoring my cousin for now, I matched the devil's gaze in the rearview mirror. I could see him reaching out toward me, his arm trembling. He was sinking into the aged fabric of the car, kinda like something out of an old *Looney Tunes* cartoon. On the floorboard beside him, the chicken proceeded to start clucking up a damn storm. It wasn't havin' all this bullshit.

"Salt ring," I said flatly, hiding my adrenaline pretty well, I thought. The food coma probably helped with that. "Under the car."

Cross's eyes widened in anger, and I swear to God actual fucking flames burst from his fingertips. But his hand had reached the edge of the ring, and his grasping fiery hand couldn't draw any closer.

That didn't mean he couldn't just light my car on fire, though.

"Break . . . it."

"Get fucked," I said, pushing my foot down harder. One hand on the wheel, I threw up the other in a one-finger salute. The engine was starting to scream, and I knew that this car was too old to take this kind of punishment for long, but I would gladly sacrifice this car to get me out of this bind. I could do without a car. But my soul? Yeah, I needed that.

Jackie was playing mental catch-up. "The keys!"

I ignored him. "This goes one of two ways. Either you go back where you came from, or we sit here until this car catches fire or the engine blows. Then we just ditch you here. Either way, your trip with us ends here."

My cousin got out of the car before Cross could respond, slamming the door shut. I glanced that way and saw him backing away from the car, his eyes locked on Cross. I didn't blame him, but damn, I would've liked a little moral support.

Cross lowered his flaming hand to just above the seat. I could see the fabric start to darken and smoke. It was a clear threat, but I wasn't gonna play that game.

I called up my power, such as I had in that moment, and my own hand burst into flames. I turned to face the devil, keeping the pressure up on the gas pedal. With a snarl, I put my hand on the headrest of the passenger seat. Out of the corner of my eye, I could see it catch fire. "Shit or get off the pot, Cross. I ain't got all day."

There ain't a devil alive, I reckon, that I could put an ounce of fear into. But I think, for the briefest moment, I saw a flash of "What the fuck is wrong with this crazy shit?" on Cross's face. Then he put his hand on the seat, and it caught fire as well. I guess to see who was gonna blink first.

Well, that would have been me ninety-nine times out of a hundred, but there was more than just my life on the line. Between Jackie and Johnny, I wasn't gonna let this demon fuck hurt my friends without a fight. So, I floored it.

I could see the worn-out foam underneath Cross beginning to spring out from the burst seams around the devil. The stench of old fabric, thoroughly nicotine soaked from the decades of smokers who'd owned it before me, filled the air, threatening to choke me. It damn sure was stinging my eyes, and I was damn near certain this was how you got cancer.

"Someone . . . will . . . call . . . me . . . back," Cross fought out. "And . . .then . . .I will . . . find . . . you all . . ."

His tone told me it wasn't a threat—it was a promise. But I was ok with that. I needed him to come for me later on, when I had more time to prepare, to get ready, 'cause there was one cassette in that case I had to get.

"Best come correct, then, I reckon. But for now, kindly fuck off."

Cross managed to cut a grin that chilled me to the bone, but I'd like to think I didn't show it. He extinguished the flames on his skin, though the seat was still afire, and then with a bit of struggle took up the guitar case in both hands. "Be . . . seeing . . . you," he spat.

And then he was gone, vanished in a puff of black smoke that managed to reek of sulfur so strong, it overpowered the scent of burning car.

The chicken was still losing its goddamn mind.

Interlude: A Dream of Future Pie

Turns out Jackie-O running off like that actually worked in my favor at first. When he saw the flames, he knew that if the car was gonna survive, he was gonna have to find some water fast. However, it was also why I was no longer speaking to him.

Beneath a drain pipe, he found a bucket full of rainwater and, managing to only spill a little of it, he managed to get it poured onto the fire while I was trying to beat it out with my shirt. He ended up soaking my shirt, but since it had also caught fire, that wasn't all bad. The chicken got wet as well, and from its seat in the back it was letting its discontent be known in the form of unending angsty clucking. 'Least it sounded angsty to me. I'm no chicken whisperer, though.

But the fire was out, with only two badly charred spots in my car as a reminder of our demonic friend. With all four windows down, you could only slightly smell that sour charred foam smell. I had hopes that it might even air out completely by the time we got to where we were headed.

In all the tumult, though, my leftovers had not only fallen to the floorboard, but had gotten splashed with the water. There was no saving them, even with my exceedingly generous interpretation of the five-second rule. It was a travesty of the highest order, and I struggled to envision a world where I could ever forgive Jack.

Once the fire was out I had scooped up the soggy remains, scraping them off the floorboard back into the Styrofoam container. The pie had smeared into the floorboard, a sight so terrible, I thought I was going to cry. I didn't even try to fully clean it up, partly because I felt such a tragic fate should be left with some sort of memorial, and partly because it was already so stained that you couldn't really tell which stain was pie once it fully dried.

I said a few brief silent words over the once-delectable remains as I placed them gently into a nearby trash can. A funeral, as it were, for a dream that had died. A dream of future pie. They were the last words I spoke until we were a good thirty miles down the road.

"I mean, you got to talk to me at some point," Jackie said.

I wasn't going to take that bait, and I just sniffed with disdain instead.

"I notice we're not heading west anymore. Are you lost, or are we not going to New Orleans anymore?"

"I'm taking you back, Judas-O," I finally replied. "I don't wanna be travelin' with someone who would let their jealousy of my food overtake their sense of right and wrong. You're lucky I didn't just leave you back at the diner. Ain't a soul alive that woulda faulted me for doin' it."

"Fuckin' A, Marsh! I told you I was sorry! Like a dozen times already. I even offered to buy you a whole-ass replacement pie!" he barked. "Would you rather your car be burnt up? That would've ruined your precious fucking pie, too, and you would've been without a car!"

I bit my tongue. *Ain't no point in arguing with a fool.*

We rode in silence a few miles more till I got stuck at a four-way stop. Truth be told, I wasn't sure which way would take me back to where we'd set out from that morning. It felt crazy that we'd only been traveling a few hours when it felt like we'd done a few days' worth of livin' in that time.

"You don't know which way to go, do you?"

I just sorta looked out the side window. There was a car coming up behind us that I figured was gonna be pissed that I wasn't moving, but that was "minute from now" Marsh's problem. I wasn't gonna break my silence on account of something as insignificant as being *lost*. I knew I just had to wait long enough and Jackie would tell me. I got the patience of Job when I'm being spiteful.

The car behind us had laid on the horn for a good five seconds when Jackie-O finally broke. "Fuck! Go right!"

I turned the car to the right, rolling slowly through the four-way so I could give the car behind us a one-finger salute. They were going straight though, so I don't think they saw me, punching the gas on through in a roar of rusted exhaust. I really was in a mood.

A mile up the road, Jack spoke, and this time his voice lacked any heat. It sounded sincere, even. "Don't take me back. Ain't nothing there for me. I want to go with you, to Jubal County. I got things I can teach you, and you got things you can teach me."

"Mississippi must be a real shithole if Jubal County sounds appealing," I said after a few moments. And just like that, the anger sorta bled outta me. You bet your ass I was gonna hold a grudge, and remind him of the horror he'd perpetrated on me whenever it was relevant. But I was getting tired of feelin' riled up.

Jackie-O just shrugged a little. "Every place sucks, man, for different reasons. You just gotta find the folks you jive with, and that's what makes a place tolerable. But yeah, Mississippi ain't great."

I grunted, but didn't really say anything. What do you say to that? "Of course, come back and live in my storage shed home! It's great! I don't have a toilet or shower, so I usually just end up using the Dairy Queen bathroom, or end up washing the stink off with some baby wipes I stole from the Dollar General."

Or maybe I should've invited him to a family bar-b-que with Granny, where she's just as likely to curse you as cuss you out? Maybe tell him about how I'm pretty sure my dad would end up killing me one day if Granny don't get to it first? Detail how I knew all the best spots to score the drugs that would probably beat either one of them to the punch?

"You owe me a pie" is what I went with, because fuck it. I guess misery loves company.

"Well, I'll get you your pie, then. But I think you owe me the end of that story."

"Fair enough."

Story Time with Howard Marsh: Coming Up Only to Hold You Under

Years Ago

I tried to dig my feet into the mud, but the neck was way too strong. It pulled me along as though I weighed hardly nothing at all. Worst of all, my leg wound up brushing against one of the creature's own legs, and it instantly became stuck. That in turn led to me being totally stuck all up and down one side of my body, like a damn wiggly bug caught in flypaper.

The water was quickly rising higher up my body with every step the neck took. It was colder than I thought it would be, and I won't lie, I shrieked a little when it hit my nuts. It was just one shriek and shout among many, though, as I fought with all my might to break free. I'd have had better luck wrestling a concrete wall, for all the good it did.

The creature's breathing was ragged and labored. I could see the foam around its mouth growing in size, becoming steadily more red. It was as good as dead on its feet. I was certain that it was going to keel over at any second, trapping me beneath the water with it.

I could see Johnny ahead of us. He was treading water, as he was clearly deep enough that it would have been over his head. I thought I caught a glimpse of a dazed, ecstatic look on the man's face, but it was only for a second. I had bigger issues to worry about, like breaking free. I did see that we were heading directly for him, and I was certain the nacken was looking to drown us both at the same time.

Then the water was up over my nips, and I knew we'd be in over my head in just a couple more steps. It was now or never, I thought, and I drew up all the power I could muster. It was hard to think straight, much less focus on calling up the magic, but I felt it begin to flow into my hands. I pulled on the threads in my reach, forcing as much as I could into me, burning through the drug-fueled energy I had left.

My chin hit the water as it took another step. I had a moment of mid-blinding panic as my body focused on just taking in as deep a breath as I could. I knew with all the smoking I did that my lungs were pretty much fucked; I was going to have to be quick, or I'd be dead in no time. I managed to choke in one solid breath before my head was underwater.

In the murkiness, I could hardly see more than the pale hide of the horselike creature, but I didn't need to see it; it was just on the end of my arms. It was a target impossible to miss, but my fingers were stuck in place, and my mouth was submerged. I had only ever managed to cast my little fireball spell by mouthing and twisting my fingers just so.

I tried to make it work without them, but I'd never done it before. The panic running through my brain wasn't helping as I tried to focus even a little bit. I could feel the foot attached to my stuck leg sinking into the mud as the beast kept stalking forward, and any hope I had of us possibly floating up was washed away. Whatever this thing was, it was heavy, and not at all buoyant.

And I was a goner if I didn't figure out how to cast a spell without speaking it.

My brain was doing the mental equivalent of frantically grasping at straws, darting around from thought to thought in a maddening cavalcade, trying an idea and immediately discarding it a fraction of a heartbeat later. My lungs were already beginning to hurt, and it had only been a few seconds. I swore I'd give up smoking if I only survived this.

I meant it, too.

INTERLUDE: GOT A LIGHT?

"Light this for me, will ya?" I asked, thumping out one of my last smokes from a mightily battered pack.

Jackie-O obliged, so I got back to telling the tale.

Story Time with Howard Marsh: An Offer That Can't Be Refused

Years Ago

The only sign that we'd reached Johnny was a little more disturbance in the water, no doubt from his paddling. But that was only for a second, at most, before I took a foot to the head. It wasn't a full kick, but it was enough to jar me—and open my mouth.

I didn't breathe in a full lung's worth of water, but I definitely swallowed more than I ever would've wanted. The water tasted earthy and dank, like a well gone sour, and it left my mouth coated with a thick film. I wanted to gag, but I knew doing so would only make it worse. I fought back the reflex as best I could.

Johnny was now caught up beside me. He was stuck along the length of the beast's head and neck, his feet having ended up glued next to one of my hands. He wasn't squirming and fighting, though, not that I could see. I figured he was still entranced. I was sure he hadn't had time to take a breath like me.

Not that mine was doing me much good. The blow to my head had robbed me of what little air I had left, and my vision was starting to turn black around the edges. My lungs were burning, and I could feel my heart pounding hummingbird quick. I was going under, and I knew that would be it for me.

That's when I got mad.

This was all so fucking *stupid.* Why did everything around me always have to go to shit?! I wanted to scream out loud but instead I just shrieked in my mind, a rage fueled by too much coke and too little luck. I fueled the last of my consciousness into it as my vision began to fully fade to black. With my dying thought, I screamed out one last "FUCK!" into the void, lashing the universe with one last curse.

My magic exploded from my palms in a blast of pure power.

The force of it blew huge chunks from the ribs of the neck, gouging holes big enough that my torso could've fit in them. The water became a slew of meat chunks and red-black water, a swirling mess that made it even harder to see. The shock of it had broken me free, and I was finally able to reach down to where my leg was still stuck. With my rapidly failing consciousness still looming, I managed somehow to blast my leg free.

Even through the dark water I was able to tell which way was up, a faint glow of sunlight shining a few feet above my head. With a couple of thrusts upwards my head broke the surface, and I gasped in a couple of deep breaths. I was still fighting to keep from passing out, but I had managed to turn the corner, I knew. The shore wasn't far off, and I knew I could easily enough struggle my way over there. I even started to try, when I quickly realized that Johnny hadn't bubbled up beside me.

What had bubbled up was a frothy mix of red water and chunks of dead horse . . . thing. It smelled fucking awful, and it made the swampy abyss even darker. I tried looking down to see if I could spot Johnny, but through all the gore I couldn't even see the paleness of the neck. It must have sunken deeper when I killed it. Killed it a second time, I guess.

I really did consider just swimming away. After all, Johnny had brought this all on himself—I told him it would end badly, and he hadn't wanted to listen, and I damn sure didn't want to swim through fairy-horse chum. But some cursed little sliver buried deep in me wouldn't let me just swim off like that. So, taking as deep a breath as I could muster, I dove back under the water.

Somehow, I didn't immediately bob back to the surface to puke, but it was a close thing. Instead I managed to choke the bile down, and with a few kicks of my legs I was able to see an outline of the neck. The pond thankfully wasn't all that deep; otherwise, I don't think I could've made it even this close.

The carcass was settling onto the bottom instead of floating up, which me think that the bones must be heavy as all hell. Otherwise, it would have come up . . . right? I didn't have a clue. I was honed in on Johnny, who I could see was still sticking to the thing. As I got close enough to see his face clearly, I could see that he was either unconscious or already dead. I was praying the former, but betting the later.

One of his arms was floating up, and I grabbed onto it. Not having to kick to keep myself down made things a little easier, but my lungs were already aching. I had to be quick or we were both probably done for.

I didn't have a real clue how I did what I'd done earlier, but I knew that I could by reflex if things got bad enough. So, I tried to think about how it had felt as I pulled myself down closer to the water horse. I captured that feeling in my mind, started to call up my power, and, with my palm outstretched, tried to replicate it. I held my hand in such a way that I hoped the blast would only hit the carcass—I didn't want to think about what might happen if Johnny was caught in the crossfire.

At first, nothing happened. Which made me mad as hell . . . and I guess that was the missing piece. It wasn't as powerful as before, but a blast launched out, mostly freeing Johnny's leg. But my lungs were screaming and I knew I didn't have the time I needed to get him free that way, not without risking hitting him, too.

So instead, I just kept blasting more or less in the same spot, and instead of freeing him from the body, I freed the body from its head. Finally, that made Johnny and such light enough that I was able to start dragging him up to the surface. I just had to swim through a nightmare swirl of horse parts to do it.

Fuck my life.

ON THE ROAD AGAIN

"Jaysus," Jackie-O said as I finished. That was his favorite word, I reckoned. "And you got him to shore, yeah?"

I nodded. "Yeah. Had to do mouth-to-mouth, but he lived."

"I bet he was pissed at you! I know I would be."

"Well, you'd be wrong there," I spat. "Johnny's a good guy, and he saw that it wasn't really my fault. And he appreciated me saving his life. We're actually pretty tight these days. Hell, you'll meet him at some point, I'm sure, iff'n you end up actually hangin' 'round Jubal County any length of time."

"Fuckin' wild, man," my cousin muttered, shaking his head a little.

Memory Lane with Howard Marsh: The Cavalry

Years Ago

I can't say I blamed Johnny for having a full-blown come apart.

You probably would, too, if you came to with a meth-mouth fool giving you mouth-to-mouth . . . and then discovered you were stuck to the severed head of the mythical creature that had tried to kill you. I'm not sure which part had him more put out, to be fair.

It took some doing, but I finally got him calmed down enough that I could leave him alone long enough to go get his phone out of his truck. Shit was proper fucked, and I had to call the only person I knew that could help. And I knew I was gonna pay for it.

After I made the call, I slunk back to where Johnny was and almost had a come apart of my own. I had made a livin' out of avoiding Granny as much as possible, and the idea of actually calling her in . . . well, I knew I was gonna catch hell.

Johnny didn't have anything to say to me that bears repeatin'. He was none too pleased with me, and honestly I wasn't wanting much to do with him, either. He'd almost gotten me killed, and brought down a whole heap of trouble into my lap to boot. So it was a mighty awkward silence there on the shores of that little pond, me on a stump, Johnny lying on the ground with a weird sorta horse head stuck to his shoulder.

"You're so stupid that if brains were dynamite, you couldn't blow your nose," said a voice from directly behind me about an hour later.

I jumped and shouted, being caught totally unawares. Granny was a sneaky shit when she wanted to be. On my feet, I whipped around to look at her.

There she was, five-foot-nothin' and wrinkled up like a prune. Her long white hair was pulled back in a loose knot tied off with a leather thong that I was certain I didn't want to know what sort of hide it was made from. She had on a faded blue blouse that you could hardly see for all the charms and amulets she wore around her neck. It was like the most hick Mardi Gras you ever saw, except for the fact that they were mostly made of crow skulls and teeth, all covered in glyphs.

Granny didn't hardly leave her house anymore. She had enough crows to handle her spyin', I reckoned, so on the rare occasion that she did, she loaded up on every charm and doodad she could carry. In one hand she had a staff about six inches taller than her, and the other clutched a plastic Walmart sack filled with other plastic sacks.

"I . . . uh . . ."

"Shut it," she snarled, striding past me with a whisper of her dress. "And don't you talk, either," she added toward Johnny. "The two of you are dumb as a box of hammers, and nowhere near as useful. So I'll thank you to shut the hell up and let me work."

I kept my mouth shut. Anyone else, I'd have taken that as a challenge to run my mouth, but the woman had me by the shorthairs, and she knew it.

She walked right over to Johnny and looked him over. She took to muttering under her breath, and from behind her like I was I could see that her arms were moving some sorta way. Whenever she worked magic around me, she was always careful to make sure I couldn't see or hear anything useful. As if I wanted to know anything like the black magic she was usually working, anyway.

As she muttered, she started poking that head with her staff. It starting peeling off of Johnny, though from the sounds of things it hurt like a motherfucker. A sort of cooked flesh smell filled the air, like ruined pork on a grill, and it set me to coughing.

But by the time I'd finished my coughing fit, Johnny was free. He jumped to his feet, leaving the head on the ground. It was clear he was about to take off running, but Granny wasn't havin' that. Her hand lashed out, and she fucking fish-hooked him. She had to reach just to get to his mouth, but she had his face pulled down to her level in a heartbeat. He started to raise his hands—no doubt to smack her so he could break free—but he fucked up when he looked into her eyes.

He froze in place like some critter caught in the hypnotic eyes of a cartoon snake. His whole body just locked in place, and that blow never landed. Instead he just locked eyes with her, staring into the face of evil.

I don't know what she said—this was her most prized and secret magic—but after about two minutes, she turned him loose. He sort of shook his head like he was dazed, scooped up his fiddle, and sorta staggered off toward the direction of his ride. Didn't even look my way.

"He won't remember anything of note," Granny said once he was out of earshot. She had pulled out an antler-handled skinning knife and was starting to hunch down beside that head. I saw the runes running down its length flash red for a moment, then she took to cutting it up and tossing the more useful chunks in a plastic bag.

She filled a couple bags part way up, real light-like, and with a snap of her fingers, a couple of crows flew down and scooped them up. How they knew where to go, I haven't the faintest, but they just flapped away a moment later. She did a few more minutes of cutting, filling up a few more bags. "You said the rest of this thing is down in that pond?"

"Yeah . . ." I started to mumble.

"Speak up, boy! Say it with your chest," she barked, not bothering to look at me.

"Yessum! Down on the bottom."

Straightening, she stepped over to the edge of the shore. Holding out her knife in my direction, she spat. "Well, I reckon you're gonna have to bring it up in chunks, then. Can't let it go to waste."

When I didn't immediately move, she cut a pointed look at the blade that got me started.

"And get after it. I don't got all damn day."

Epilogue: What a Long, Strange Trip It's Been

Y ou've made it this far, and what a wild ride it has been. Thank you for sticking with it.

This book marks the end of the first third of the Redemption of Howard Marsh. Six books of mistakes and mischief, coupled with far too many drugs and curses. The first arc of the saga is now complete. There are two more arcs to come, and your reward for getting this far is a hint of what's to come.

Marsh has begun to climb out from the gutter, and though he has a long way to go, he has begun to build the adoptive family that will help him. You might call this finished arc Found Hope, and in that case, the arc to come could be summarized as Found Family. By the end of it, he may even use that support to try and get clean. Just bear in mind that even free of his addictions, our hero is still a contrary redneck.

And of course, there are a number of circling forces that have taken notice of our favorite methgician. Powers beyond his ability to handle—at least for now. These are the kind of foes it will take all the help March can muster to defeat.

In the hidden places between the worlds, a devil curses his name and waits for someone to call him back to Earth.

Below the surface of a river beyond space and time, a catfish god lurks, yet to call in a favor owed.

Somewhere out there a murderous father hides from the law, no doubt biding his time until it is safe to seek revenge against the son who wronged him.

Does the briar witch still plot her revenge? Her plans are ever churning, stirring up memories and secrets better left long buried.

There is also the distant rumble of engines, signaling new horrors that are set to roll into the County and bring with it a whole new type of trouble.

And at the heart of it all, there is Granny. Her grandson has drawn her eye, and nothing good will come of it—of that, you can be certain.

<h1 style="text-align:center">THE BACK MATTER!</h1>

About the Author

Born and raised in South Alabama, Bob is an author, podcaster, tabletop game designer, and all around hot mess. His cause of death will most likely result from one of the hitchhikers with he picks up reckless abandon. A study in contrasts, he once skinny-dipped at a wedding and is also an Eagle Scout. He has two useless college degrees, has roadied for bands, and broke his wrist in a wall of death at a Divine Heresy show. He's written for video games, designed board games, and owns a disturbing number of roleplaying games. When he was eight he give a camel a coke in Israel and got flashed in Paris. When he grew up he watched a monkey steal a man's wallet in Costa Rica. He's made passible podcasts, filmed terrible short horror movies, and been the producer on a trio of albums you've never heard of. Thriving on the groans of those he has punned around he spends far too much time nervously laughing. He once dug up a dead cow in a creek thinking it was a human cadaver and has a cousin that's a water witch. In college he gave haunted ghost tours (even though he's pretty sure ghosts aren't real). He's been stalked, gave a Prophet a lift, and been stagger drunk in more states than he would care to admit.

Growing up, he was always jealous of the wide variety of jobs his favorite authors listed in their 'about the author' sections, not fully realizing what a hellscape he was lusting after. So to that end Bob has been in no particular order: a warehouse clerk, a roadie for a band, pizza delivery guy, grocery store bag boy, telephone survey giver, inventory manager, quit Walmart after only three days, and currently works in IT. Learn from him sweet children, and flee now to the woods and leave behind the world of men.

More relevant he wrote this book, some other books, and has been published by a number of other folks with questionable judgement. The fictional things he writes sometimes come weirdly true. He lives in the middle of Alabama with his amazing LadyWife, the Kiddo, and a number of increasingly portly cats.

You can learn more at **www.talesbybob.com**

Reviews!

Did you leave a review? In the immortal words of Mathew McConaughey: "It'd be a lot cooler if you did."

Email List!

If you want to keep up with news about my books, this is the best way! I'll never sell or share my email list, and I promise to never bother you more than once a month (unless, like, its super-mega-secret important). To sign up go to my website: **www.talesbybob.com**

Patreon!

If you want even more Bob content, then go check out his Patreon. It's full of short stories, flash fictions, even draft copies of books. Big news also gets announced there before anywhere else, along with sneak peaks of book covers and other behind the scenes content. A popular series on there are 'The Marsh Dispatches' which is an ongoing series of essays written from the perspective of Howard Marsh the Methgician. Check out **www.patreo n.com/talesbybob**

Transparency!

When I started out, I had no other authors that I knew well enough to ask questions about sales numbers, social media growth, etc. I had no idea if my sales numbers were good, bad, or somewhere in-between. But seeing as I'm a big believer in the concept of *'be the change you want to see'* I started sharing all that information in hopes that it would motivate other authors to do the same. And even if they don't, at least this information is available to anyone who wants to know what those types of stats look like for a small time author like myself. So if you visit my website you can see all sorts of behind the scenes information each month, like how my social media grew (or shrank), how sales were, what I tried differently that month, etc. I also break down my stats around my book launches and get into the nitty gritty of each major in person event I do. Check out **www.talesbybob.com/transparency-project**

Education!

I have been helped by countless other creatives and authors along my journey. So anything I can do to pay that help forward, I do. That's why as much as possible I try to keep a host of free resources on my website folks to learn from. If I get paid to teach a workshop, I usually turn it into a youtube video and share the powerpoint I used along with it. If I get asked the same question enough times I will turn it into a blog post or video. I also offer up 'intern' opportunities for folks who want to learn in person sales. And if you want something more in depth, check out my book "Create Your Way to Freedom! How

To Be A Big Success From Someone Who Isn't!" Check out **www.talesbybob.com/education**

Podcasts!

Bob does a lot podcasting. You should go to his website, **www.talesbybob.com** (noticing a theme here?), and check them out. Most of them are related to books in some way, but not all! His best known historically has been Books, Beards, Booze.

Book Clubs!

Want to read this book as part of your book club? Reach out! If you are close enough, I might come speak to it (especially if yall have good snacks). If you are farther away, I might be available to speak to your group remotely. At the bare minimum I will shoot you an email with some bonus content of some sort, and some book club discussion questions. Just us the contact form on my website, **www.talesbybob.com/contact**

About Bearded Bard Inkworks

A real human book publisher, who puts out novels and ttrpgs!

Here at Bearded Bard Inkworks, we are human people, who put out books, and things like books. Booky things. With actual pages. And ink. Except when they're digital of course. Either way, we're absolutely people, and not at all three octopuses pretending to be book publishers. Just look at the top hats. Only a human could be so fashionable.

Look, we love books here at Bearded Bard Inkworks. We do. But we also love rpgs. And general weirdness. So we seek out authors who are exploring unique spaces, while also generating cool tabletop games. Because who doesn't love the idea of finding that next book they love, and then getting to play a game in that world?

Learn more at **www.beardedbardinkworks.com**

Struggling with Drug Addiction?

If you or someone you know is struggling with drug addiction and want to get help, then call the number below. It is the Substance Abuse and Mental Health Services Administration help line, a confidential, free, 24-hour-a-day, 365-day-a-year, information service, in English and Spanish, for individuals and family members facing mental and/or substance use disorders. This service provides referrals to local treatment facilities, support groups, and community-based organizations. Callers can also order free publications and other information.

1-800-662-HELP (4357)

For more information you can visit their website here:

www.samhsa.gov/